Smiley pulled his head out of Nan's arms and snarled, and the team backed off hurriedly. His long dagger teeth slashed through the air, narrowly missing them.

"Nan!" Ailee said urgently. "The tranquilizer they gave you? Smiley needs it now!"

Will added quietly, "The beast hath tasted man's blood, Nan. Observe him."

Smiley crouched by the airlock's outer doors. The saber-teeth were red-tipped with Milo Pike's blood. As she watched, the pink tongue flicked out and licked the teeth clean. His golden cat's eyes closed lazily, then blinked open again, watching Nan.

She felt her skin prickling with fear.

Shakily, Nan took a step toward Smiley. In her pocket, her right hand closed over the small jet spray syringe that contained the animal tranquilizer.

"Good boy, Smiley," she said. Her fingers were slippery with sweat and awkward around the syringe. She fumbled, then plunged the needle into a fold of skin behind his ear. "You're the best."

Smiley's yellow eyes glared at her, his tail flicked to and fro like an angry cat's. She took a slow step back, watching him, then another.

"Did you get him?" Ailee whispered.

She turned to face Ailee. "I think so—"

And Smiley sprang.

Nan went down.

Ailee screamed.

DAVID BRIN'S
OUT OF TIME
TIGER IN THE SKY

SHEILA FINCH

CREATED BY DAVID BRIN

AVON BOOKS  NEW YORK

This is a work of fiction. Names, characters, places, and incidents either are the product of the author's imagination or are used fictitiously. Any resemblance to actual events, locales, organizations, or persons, living or dead, is entirely coincidental and beyond the intent of either the author or the publisher.

AVON BOOKS, INC.
1350 Avenue of the Americas
New York, New York 10019

Copyright © 1999 by Sheila Finch
"Out of Time" is a trademark of David Brin
Library of Congress Catalog Card Number: 98-94939
ISBN: 0-380-79971-5
www.avonbooks.com

First Avon Books Printing: July 1999

AVON BOOKS TRADEMARK REG. U.S. PAT. OFF. AND IN OTHER COUNTRIES, MARCA REGISTRADA, HECHO EN U.S.A.

Printed in the U.S.A.

WCD 10 9 8 7 6 5 4 3 2 1

*For Shannon, Kyle, Austin,
Autumn, Douglas, and Christopher,
with love.*

"Phone call for you, Nan," Mrs. Turner announced. "Remember good telephone etiquette and don't talk too long!"

Nan Smith made a face, but the House Mother was heading back to her office and didn't see it.

"Yeah?" Nan growled into the receiver. Her mom wouldn't call this late on a Friday evening. So it was probably her social worker making sure she hadn't run away from Oak House like she'd run away from home. Next time she did, the social worker had warned her, she'd be sent to Juvenile Hall.

"Nan?" her ten-year-old brother's voice said.

"What do you want, Ti?" Nan said. "You have to do your own homework now. I can't help you."

"This isn't about homework," Ti said. "Grampa's sick. I heard Mom on the phone today, talking to the lady at the convalescent home. Mom thinks he might be dying."

Grampa dying? Nan couldn't believe it! She'd visited him a few Sundays ago. He'd showed her how to read the *I Ching* hexagrams, the Chinese way of telling fortunes. Her grandfather had come from China a long time ago to run a martial arts school in town. Trouble never seemed so bad when Grampa

1

Hong was around. What would she do without him?

"I'll try and go see him," she said. But she didn't know how she was going to get out of Oak House to do it.

"Too bad you can't just beam over, like they do on the *Enterprise*!" Ti said. "Hurry up and get out of there so we can go to the movies again, okay?"

Nan hung up the phone. She turned to find two other girls waiting behind her. Tank, the heavy one, had her shirt sleeves rolled way up to show off her tattoos.

The other one, a thin girl with straggly blonde hair that looked as if she'd poured the Clorox bottle on it, scowled at Nan. "You took long enough!" she grumbled.

"Use smoke signals next time, Indian," Tank said.

Nan moved to pass them. She didn't want these two as enemies, but if they insisted, she'd be ready. At the last second, Tank stuck out a foot to trip her. As she stumbled, Nan twisted round and caught Tank in the middle with her elbow. Recovering, she grabbed the girl with her other hand and tumbled her to the floor.

"Ouch!" Tank wailed. "I'll get you for that, Smith!"

Nan went upstairs to the small bedroom she shared with Consuela Gonzalez. Connie was in her pajamas, listening to a Selena tape and doing her nails. Nan could smell the pear odor of the polish as soon as she came through the door.

"You look as if somebody kicked you!" Connie said, glancing up from the bright pink bottle.

The tabby house cat, Tiger, was washing himself in the middle of Nan's bed. She dropped facedown beside him and flung one arm over him. He was her only friend, always choosing her bed to sleep on.

"I've got to get out of here. I hate being stuck in this place," she said.

"Don't we all." Connie sighed.

"Yeah. But I'm going to be fifteen in another couple of months."

Nan sat up and stared out the window. Their room was at the front of Oak House looking over the quiet Santa Marta street. Somehow she had to slip out so she could visit Grampa and get back again before the House Mother noticed she was gone, or they'd send her off to Juvie for sure.

"You're getting a bad record," Connie said. "Mrs. Turner says a bad record will ruin your future."

Nan picked up a brush from the chest of drawers between the two beds and began to smooth out her long black hair.

"I don't have a future," she argued. "Mom's new boyfriend says I'm not going anyplace. He says Ti and I are just mutts because we're part Chinese, part Irish-American, part Native American on my dad's side—"

Connie interrupted. "Can't you go live with your dad?"

"No, I can't. He died when I was six," Nan said. "Mom's second husband raised us. That's how come we use his last name. But he split a year ago. All I remember of my real dad was he gave us long names, Shenandoah and Ticonderoga."

"I'm sorry," Connie said. "Not about the names. They're nice."

Nan shook her head. "They're too long."

Mom's new boyfriend did drugs, which was one of the reasons Nan had left home. But she didn't want to rat on him to the cops because it would get her

3

mom in trouble too. So she'd been sent to Oak House.

Tiger swatted at the hairbrush and she stroked him again. Some days she thought cats were better than people. They understood her moods and she understood them and their needs.

"I'm going to be a nurse when I leave school," Connie announced. "What're you going to be?"

When she was a little kid, Nan had thought about being a veterinarian; it would be kind of nice to make sick animals healthy again. But going to vet college meant staying in school, staying out of trouble, and getting good grades right now. That was hard to do when she kept getting suspended for fighting.

"I hate school," Nan said. "The teachers are dorks, the girls are snobs, and the guys are jerks. So what's the use?"

"It's not *that* bad," Connie said. "You're exaggerating."

"And it gets worse," Nan said. "You see every night on TV how bad things are. Drugs. Gangs. Riots. Murders. None of us has a future. Not you, not me—"

"I'm not going to listen!" Connie grabbed her toothbrush and toothpaste and stalked out of the bedroom, banging the door.

Nan took the Selena tape out. Then she went back to her new problem. She had no friends, and other than her brother, Ti, Grampa was the only person she cared about. She had to find a way to go see him. Yes, a matter transporter would be nice, but that only happened in the movies. She had to find her own way to get around.

A city bus ran past the corner of the street. That would take her downtown, and a transfer would get her to Grampa's convalescent home on the other side of Santa Marta. If she waited until it got really dark, she could climb out the window onto the porch roof and down to the street. She hoped the buses ran late. If not, she'd spend the night at the bus station and catch one early in the morning. It wouldn't be the first time she'd slept on a bench someplace.

Maybe she just wouldn't come back at all. Everybody here expected her to end up in Juvie anyway. Why not just cut out now and avoid all the scenes? She was tough; she didn't need anybody's help. She could make it on her own.

What about Ti? She couldn't help him stuck in here anyway. Besides, he was old enough now to start taking care of himself.

If she waited till it got completely dark, Connie would be back in the room, but she didn't want to get her roomie into trouble. With luck Connie would think she'd gone to the other bathroom when she found the room empty, then she'd fall asleep, and nobody would find out Nan had gone until morning.

Better go now and take the risk of being seen by the House Mother or one of the counselors who might come out of the house. She opened the drawer and pulled out a warm red sweater. Her purse lay under it; she'd need a couple of dollars for bus fare. Something else she couldn't leave behind: a flashlight Ti had given her last Christmas. It might be useful.

Then she carefully slid the bedroom window up. It squealed in the track, and she waited, but nobody came running. It was easy enough to climb out. Close it again, she thought, or Connie'll know right away where I went. The porch roof seemed to buckle under her weight and she worried that it might give way. Two steps took her to the edge, where she sat down, turned around, and lowered her legs over the edge.

She landed with a bump in a flower bed at the side of the porch step. Holding her breath, she waited for a moment. Nobody came out to see what the noise was.

Walking fast, but not so fast she attracted attention, Nan headed for the bus stop.

Yeah, she thought. Shenandoah Whitecrow, aka Nan Smith, had a lot of practice in looking after herself.

2

It was much too nice a Saturday afternoon to be indoors, practicing. Jerry Vanderburg carefully laid down his cello against the antique table. He flicked a strand of light brown hair off his forehead.

He was tired of the cello. Not of music, because he loved that. But he'd have preferred one of the horns, trombone maybe, or the trumpet, something he could use in the marching band. If he wasn't allowed to play football, at least he could play with the band. But his mother wouldn't hear of it. Seemed like she was never going to forget he'd had leukemia as a little kid.

Jerry looked out the long, open French windows at the garden. Rufus, his Irish Setter, was chasing butterflies on the grass. What he wanted to do was go down to the park where Jim and Luis and the others were playing baseball, but that would've upset his mother too; she was still afraid he'd overexert himself and get sick again. In his mind he could hear the soft *thock* of the ball as someone hit it, and he could almost smell that warm, incense smell of a fall afternoon outdoors.

Nobody was home. Mom, an environmental lawyer, was out of town, and Dad had gone into the lab even though it was Saturday. His father was a scientist at the Jet Propulsion Laboratory in Pasadena; he smashed atoms and studied particles and did some cool research stuff on space.

Everybody expected Jerry to be a scientist too one day. His parents even had a university picked out for him to attend: Cal Tech, because it was close enough that he could live at home and wouldn't wear himself out traveling, his mom said. Nobody had asked him where he wanted to go or what he wanted to study. Science was like music. Jerry liked it and was good at it, but he was fifteen now and he wished his parents would leave him alone to make his own choices.

And he wished they'd stop trying to protect him against everything. If they had their way, he'd grow up in a cocoon and never hatch out because it might be dangerous. Just once in his life he'd like to do something exciting and maybe a bit risky, not the boring, safe things his parents planned.

He made up his mind and put the cello away in its padded case. Whistling for Rufus to come with him, he stepped out through the glass doors and headed to the garage at the bottom of the garden. Other kids in his class had their learner's permits right now, he thought, glancing at his mother's car. He was taking driver's ed, but his mom wouldn't have let him practice even if he'd had his permit. He'd have to take his bike.

It wasn't till he was on the saddle of his silver racing bike that he remembered the guys had talked about trying a new park on the other side of town. "That's a bad area," Jim had said. But Luis had argued, "Yeah, but it's got a brand new fancy sports complex."

The new park shouldn't be difficult to find. Just take State Street all the way across Santa Marta. If he couldn't find it, he could always ask at a gas station. Cycling sure beat practicing the cello on a nice day like this.

"Come on, Rufe!" he yelled.

The big red dog came running to him.

State Street went on for miles, slowly getting narrower and losing the tree-lined center divider. Mom would really throw a fit if she knew how far he'd cycled, and where. The neighborhoods of two-story houses with big yards gave way to rows of apartment buildings and shabby strip malls. Then Jerry realized that State Street was going to run out altogether in another half block. He could see the dead-end sign up ahead, and he could hear the noise of a freeway.

He'd never been to this part of town before. The street was lined with old warehouses that had windows boarded up and graffiti sprayed on them. Someone had shot out most of the street lamps. The sidewalk looked as if the street cleaners never came to this end of town; scraps of paper blew about, and cigarette butts were everywhere. And Jerry thought it stank as bad as the public toilets at the park the morning after a three-day weekend.

He cycled carefully, avoiding broken glass in the street, searching for a gas station where he could get directions. He'd just about decided to go back home when he noticed two teenagers leaning against a wall, smoking. They had shaved heads and tattoos, and they were looking at Jerry as if he'd just landed from Mars. Gang members. Definitely not the people to ask.

"Rufus, come!" he called, turning around.

But Rufus had spotted a cat, and the goofy dog chose that moment to chase it. The gray cat ran straight toward the two guys, and the dog ran right after it. At the last minute, the cat swerved and darted down a narrow alley between two buildings with Jerry's Irish setter in hot pursuit.

He had to follow Rufus and try to catch him before the dog got hopelessly lost. The two guys up ahead watched with interest. Jerry picked up speed, then leaned the bike over and skidded as fast as he could around the corner of the building after his dog.

A hand shot out and grabbed his arm as he went by. Jerry and the bike tumbled to the street

"Cool bike," one guy commented.

"Always wanted one like that," the other guy said.

Jerry looked up into two hard, mean faces. They were not much older than he was, he guessed, but that was where the similarity between them ended.

"Let me go, please. I've got to find my dog," Jerry said.

The first guy said, "Hear that, Blade? He gotta find his doggie. Please let him go! Ain't that somethin'?"

"Too bad, punk," the one called Blade snarled. "This here's our turf."

"I didn't mean to come here. I was looking for the park." But he realized it was useless arguing with them.

Blade was holding something behind his back. "Tell you what. Gimme the bike an' I'll let you go."

"No way!" As soon as the words were out, Jerry knew it was the wrong thing to say.

Blade's arm flashed into view holding a broken baseball bat. It struck Jerry on the side of his head and he stumbled to his knees. The pain was sharp and burning. His ears were ringing.

"That was dumb, punk," Blade said.

From the corner of his eye, Jerry saw the other teen

pick up the bike. He struggled to stand up.

"Leave that alone!" he shouted.

Blade's boot kicked him hard in the stomach, and he went down again, sprawled out on the sidewalk.

3

Grampa Hong was lying very still with a white sheet pulled up under his chin when Nan came into his room at the convalescent hospital. His eyes were closed and white hair straggled across the pillow. He looked like a stranger.

"Grampa?" she said.

She was afraid she'd come too late. It had taken longer than she'd hoped to catch the right bus across Santa Marta. But then he opened his eyes, the strangeness fell away, and her own Grampa looked out at her again.

She remembered the Chinese he'd taught her and said hello. *"Ni hao!"*

Grampa said, "I knew you'd come."

"How're you feeling?" she asked.

"Fine." Grampa nodded at her. "But how are you doing, my Shenandoah?"

"I'm in a lot of trouble." She sat down on his bed. "And I just ran away again."

"Do you remember what the fifth hexagram of the *I Ching* told you?" Grampa asked, his wrinkled old fingers smoothing her hair.

"Don't give up even if you fall in the mud," she said. "Something like that."

Grampa smiled. "Light and success if you are sincere. In the end, there will be good fortune."

She thought he knew the whole *I Ching* book by heart. "That might work for a Chinese emperor, Grampa. But I'm just a dumb Indian."

"Your father would never have said that," he scolded. "He was a good man. He told me his people tried to walk in beauty, and that's something I understand."

Grampa had been teaching her his philosophy for as long as she could remember. He'd taught her and Ti the Chinese martial art, kung fu. "But this is not so you can go out and hurt people," he'd warned them. "Kung fu is a way of living, not killing." He wouldn't approve of her fighting in school if he knew, but sometimes she didn't see any other way of getting through the bad stuff that kept happening.

"Time for your pills, Mr. Hong," said a nurse's aide in a white uniform. She stood in the doorway, holding a tray with a tiny paper cup.

Nan's grandfather had never used Western medicine. He made teas from leaves and flowers. Watching him now, obediently swallowing pills, made a lump come up in Nan's throat.

The woman turned to Nan. "Don't stay too long and get him overtired."

The aide went out of the room, and as soon as she did, Grampa put his hand to his mouth and took out two pills. He put them in a tissue and dropped them in the waste basket beside his bed.

Nan laughed. Grampa laughed too. And then for some reason Nan's laughter turned to tears. Grampa held her close, and she could feel his bony ribs under the thin pajama top. He smelled of soap and talcum powder.

"You have things to do in your life, Shenandoah," he said. "An important path to follow. The *I Ching* is never wrong."

He looked very old and worn out. She leaned down and kissed him on the cheek.

"Goodbye, Grampa," she said. "I'll come again as soon as I can."

His eyes were closed, but he waggled his fingers at her.

Nan walked slowly out of the convalescent home that afternoon feeling older than when she walked in. She didn't believe in Chinese prophecies.

The convalescent home was in a run-down, noisy part of Santa Marta. The bus stop was several blocks away. There was trash everywhere, and she'd forgotten how bad this area smelled. Oak House almost seemed like Beverly Hills by comparison, but she wasn't going back there. She knew she was making a real mess out of her life, but she couldn't see how to fix it. She walked aimlessly for a while, trying not to think too hard.

A gray cat streaked past her ankles, followed by a large red dog that almost bowled her over. Both animals disappeared. She looked around. She didn't recognize this street. Great! She'd gotten herself lost.

Suddenly she heard shouting around the corner. Someone needed help. Nan started running.

She turned the corner just in time to see a teenager strike a thin kid who was trying to hold on to a racing bike. That boy toppled over, and the teen kicked him. Another teen hopped on the saddle.

"Hey!" she yelled.

The teen pedaled away fast. The first one ran after him.

Nan hurried over to the fallen kid who was clutching his stomach. "You okay?" she asked.

He had light brown hair and pale skin that looked as if he didn't get out much, but other than a nasty bump on the side of his head he didn't seem too badly hurt.

"Thank you," he said in a hoarse voice.

"We should get away from here fast," Nan said. "Can you stand?"

He looked at her and she saw his eyes were dark blue. "I think so."

"I'll help." She held out her hand. "Name's Nan."

"Jerry." He got up slowly. "I think I twisted my ankle. And my stomach feels terrible."

"We'd better get to the bus stop. Where do you live, Jerry?"

"I can't leave. My dog's around here somewhere," he said.

"Big red one?" Nan asked. "I saw it. We'll look for it as we walk."

Jerry leaned against her as they took slow steps forward. At this rate, she thought, they'd still be here when it got dark, which it was starting to do already.

"Rufe?" Jerry croaked. "Where are you?"

Nan knew the gang members or their homies could come back at any moment. A few street lights that hadn't been broken were starting to come on, and a liquor store's sign sputtered to life.

"Rufus!" Jerry shouted.

For a moment, Nan thought she saw the big red dog across the street, but when she looked right at it, she saw it wasn't a dog after all. And then whatever it was disappeared.

Something seemed to be happening to her ears, because she wasn't hearing anything anymore. A moment ago, the street had been noisy with the sound of cars, a police chopper overhead, dogs barking. Now it was as if she had cotton stuffed in her ears.

An odd, electric blue light seemed to be growing up out of the sidewalk at their feet. Nan stared. It got bigger and bigger and seemed to be spinning. It was making some kind of humming sound that she felt in her bones. She couldn't look away from it even if she wanted to.

The blue light looked more and more like a mouth that was opening up to swallow them. Jerry leaned into it, gazing at something. Nan was suddenly scared.

"Rufus?" Jerry said. "Bad dog! What're you doing in there?"

Nan narrowed her eyes and peered into the spinning light. It seemed to have formed a kind of tunnel now, going down through the sidewalk. She felt dizzy, sick to her stomach.

Whatever it was in there, it was dog-size and dog-color, but somehow she knew that it wasn't a dog.

"Come on, Jerry!" Nan urged. "Let's go."

Then behind her, she heard a bark, and turning her head she saw Jerry's dog racing towards them.

"I can't go without my dog!" Jerry said.

"Look!" she shouted. "There's your real dog!"

But Jerry had moved one foot forward into the hole and suddenly the light seized him. She saw him waving his arms, trying to keep from being sucked in.

"Run!" she yelled, grabbing his arm.

Too late. The light sucked her into the tunnel with him.

4

Inside the tunnel that had mysteriously appeared in the sidewalk, the blue light was dazzling. The way it flickered made Nan want to throw up. There was a peculiar smell too, like hot metal, and that didn't help.

"Do sit down," a strange voice said. "The motion sickness will pass if you don't fight it. At least, I think it will. Most people remain unconscious during the trip so I'm not really sure."

Nan couldn't even make out the floor through the bright mist. With a dry throat she murmured, "I can't see where to sit."

Jerry tugged at her sleeve, pulling her down, and she sat cross-legged beside him on a rubbery, rippling surface. The dizzy feeling faded.

"You okay?" Jerry asked.

"Yeah," Nan said. "But what happened? Where are we?"

"I think we've been grabbed by a UFO!" Jerry said.

"Oh, hardly that," the strange voice said.

Both Jerry and Nan turned to stare at the odd-looking dog she'd spotted trailing them just before she'd been sucked inside the tunnel. She had to squint through the strange mist that was still swirling around.

Actually, the thing looked just like the Irish setter that chased the cat a few minutes ago, but there was something about its eyes that made Nan shiver. For one thing, they were the wrong color, steel gray instead of brown. And ordinary dogs didn't speak.

"What's going on?" she demanded. "What're you doing to us?"

"Well," the dog-thing said, "I was sent here to get Gerald Middleton Vanderburg III, known as Jerry. He's needed, you see. And for some reason you came along too."

Jerry winced to hear the dog-thing say his whole name. But Nan thought it wasn't much worse than being called Shenandoah.

"You've got some explaining to do," she said. "And it'd better be good."

"I should introduce myself," the dog-thing said. "I'm an AI. Artificial Intelligence. A smart computer, in your terms, disguised to resemble Jerry's pet."

"Yeah, right!" Nan said scornfully. "I'll believe that!"

"I can't lie." The thing spoke calmly. "By the way, you can call me Arti. And you can think of me as a 'he.' "

"You said somebody sent you. Who?" Nan was glad nobody from Oak House was around to hear her talking to a dog, even if it claimed to be a computer. "This whole thing's crazy. Some kind of stupid joke!"

Jerry asked, "What planet are you from, Arti?"

She was about to think Jerry must've got hit worse than she'd thought, but he turned to her and winked so she would know he was just going along with the dog-thing.

"Do stop thinking of UFOs!" Arti's tongue lolled

out of his mouth just like a real dog. "Humans sent me, of course. The planet I come from is Earth in the year 2345."

"You mean the future?" Jerry's voice squeaked as if he were excited. "Is that where you're taking us?"

"Everything will be explained once we arrive," the computer-dog said. "Then you'll have a chance to decide if you want to stay."

Jerry's smile faded. "What about my dog? What'll happen to Rufus?"

"When we're done, we'll return you to a moment just one second after the one when you were yanked," Arti explained. "Your dog will still be there."

Nan found that very hard to believe. But Jerry looked satisfied; he seemed like the kind of kid who'd be a science nerd, she thought, all brain and no street smarts. Then she remembered what she'd thought yesterday, that anything would be better than Oak House. She seemed to have gotten her wish. But whatever this was, she'd better not let her guard down.

She glanced around. The mist seemed to have faded away, and now she could see one end of the tunnel of light glowing blue, the other with a reddish tint. Her stomach wasn't knotted up any more, but it was getting very warm and she was feeling sleepy. She blinked her eyes.

"It'll help to get up now and start walking," Arti suggested. "We won't get there any faster, but you won't feel as heavy if you move. It has to do with the energy build-up of sublight speed, but I don't think you'd understand the explanation."

"Try me anyway," Jerry said. He waited but Arti didn't explain, so he tried another question. "What did you mean, I'm needed? By whom? Why me?"

"Everything will be made clear when we reach 2345," Arti said.

Something very odd was happening to Nan. Suddenly she seemed to be in the middle of a large crowd of people, all arguing and pushing. She could actually feel them! Somebody near her was crying. It sounded like a little kid, but when she looked, nobody was there. She could *hear* people shouting all around her, but she couldn't *see* any of them. She knew something bad had happened. These people were very scared.

"Take it easy, Nan," Arti said. "You're just going through a minor temporal displacement effect. A kind of memory of your future."

"But I'm supposed to do something!" she cried out.

"Whatever it is you're sensing, it's not here yet. Probably not for many more years, when you've grown up," Arti said soothingly. "Don't worry about it now."

The panicky sensation passed as fast as it had started. Nan stood up, shaking. Jerry looked a little glassy-eyed too but he didn't say anything.

"Come along," Arti said. "Let's get moving."

Jerry clutched the computer-dog's collar and Nan held on to Jerry's sleeve. Together they took a few slow steps down the tunnel. The blue light at the end seemed to be rushing toward them but not getting any closer.

Nan couldn't forget the invisible crowd. If this whole crazy tunnel thing was for real, and if whatever it was that just happened was waiting for her in the future, she didn't want to go there. It was just like the bad stuff in the movies. But the computer-dog said they were going to 2345. Almost three hundred and fifty years into the future! None of this made any sense.

"Here it comes," Arti announced. "Watch your step."

Nan felt as if she'd been pushed off a moving train.

5

The bright tunnel vanished, and Jerry went sprawling onto hands and knees on something thick and white. His body felt totally wiped out like it did sometimes after an intense baseball game, the kind he didn't tell his mother about if he didn't want her shrieking about his health.

It took him a few seconds to get everything under control. Then he saw he'd landed on a carpet in a room that had a floor and walls and a ceiling—wonderfully normal by comparison with the weird tunnel, except that they were all white.

A tall, thin-faced man and a golden-haired woman wearing matching silvery jumpsuits helped Jerry over to a white couch. The minute he stood up he discovered he was going to have trouble walking. His bones seemed to have dissolved, leaving legs that wouldn't support him.

He sat down on the couch, and after a moment his head stopped spinning. He glanced over at Nan. She was getting up off the floor very slowly. It looked as if her legs might feel rubbery too, but nobody was paying her any attention.

Jerry could see two small glowing lights in a control panel on a blank wall, one red and one green.

Apart from the panel and the plain white couch, there was no other furniture in the room. The computer-dog that looked so much like Rufus sat back on its haunches and watched them.

The golden-haired woman smiled. "We need one hour of your time, Jerry. We're going to explain something quite surprising to you, then we're going to ask you to do something for us. Something *very* important. After that, we'll give you the chance to say no, and if you do, we'll see you get back safely to your home with no harm done."

"Sure," Jerry said. This might be weird, but it beat getting roughed up by gang members. "I'll listen. Go ahead."

The tall man had turned away from Jerry and was staring at Nan as if he'd just noticed her.

"Who's this?" the man asked. He glanced down at Arti. "We sent you to get Gerald Vanderburg. Not this girl."

"She grabbed him and came right along," Arti explained. The computer-dog licked a paw just like a real dog.

"Well, she'll have to go right back again!" The man took a step toward Nan. His jumpsuit sparked as if it were electric. "Serena, help her stand while I start the 'port."

The woman went over to where Nan was sitting on the carpet and looked down at her for a moment.

"Are you certain, Arlo?" the woman said. "The AIs don't usually make a mistake like this."

"Of course I'm certain, Serena!" the man snapped. "You. What's your name?"

"Me?" Nan said. "I'm Nan Smith."

"Nan Smith?" the man said sarcastically. "Nobody's ever heard of her!"

" 'Course not!" Nan said. "I haven't finished growing up yet."

Jerry sent her a thumbs up sign. Way to go! The man called Arlo had a sour expression, as if he'd been eating lemons. Not a pleasant guy at all.

Serena smiled and her green eyes sparkled. "Take my hand, Nan. You'll be okay once you get home again."

With Serena's help, Nan got to her feet. Serena was really pretty, Jerry realized, and she had a sweet voice. He kind of liked older women; they were usually more serious and knowledgeable than girls his own age.

Already Jerry's shakiness was fading away, and in its place he felt a growing excitement. He was relieved they weren't going to send him home again right away. Whatever was going on here sounded way more interesting than staying home and practicing the cello. He felt sorry for Nan, who would have to miss out.

Arlo reached out to the red light on the wall.

Then Nan pulled away from the woman with the gold hair.

"You dragged me here," Nan said. "No excuses or apologies. Not even an explanation. And now you want to send me back like something you bought that doesn't work. Well, I'm not going!"

"You have no choice," Arlo said. "I'm sorry for the inconvenience. But we don't bring people into the future just to have fun. We can't use you. Now, be a good girl and stand over there. Serena, please prepare the amnesiac."

"Arlo, aren't you taking this a bit too personally?" Serena asked. "I mean, I understand your family circumstances—"

"No!" Arlo snapped.

Serena moved away. Jerry thought she looked upset, as if she didn't approve of the guy's rudeness. What was with that guy, anyway? he wondered. Arlo seemed to be wound up tighter than a spring. Then his attention was drawn to the small control panel. Below it, he saw an electric blue hole growing, and there was a humming sound he remembered hearing once before. Serena came back holding what looked like a very thin spray bottle with a few drops of gold-colored liquid inside.

"I don't do drugs!" Nan said firmly.

"Arlo," Serena began, the bottle still unused in her hand, "perhaps—"

"No, Serena. We're too busy to play tour guides to unproven ancestors. Off you go, Nan Smith." Arlo stretched out his right hand to push Nan into the blue hole. "Try to make the best of your life."

But then a surprising thing happened. At the last second Nan caught the man's arm, twisted it, and dumped him on the carpet. He landed heavily, the air whooshing out of his lungs, and lay on his back staring up at Nan as if he couldn't believe a girl could've done it. Jerry was impressed too. In fact, if he were honest, he knew he couldn't do it himself. Maybe Nan deserved to stay if she wanted to.

"If you send my friend Nan back," Jerry said, "then I won't do anything to help you either. You have my word on that."

"Ah, they both show grit," Arti said. The computer-dog seemed to be grinning. "Just the trait you're looking for, I believe?"

Nobody moved for a few seconds. Then Serena started laughing.

"I don't see what's so funny," Arlo grumbled.

"If Nan goes, I go," Jerry added. He was sitting up on the white couch now, feeling much better. He wasn't going to let these people push either him or Nan around.

"What difference will one more on the team make?" Serena asked. "Maybe she'll be useful after all."

Arlo shook his head. "That isn't how we'd planned it."

"If I may suggest something, dear doctors," Arti said. "An overreliance on detailed plans that were supposed to make everything safe is one of the problems that made people of our time attempt this desperate gamble. Perhaps a dose of the unexpected is exactly what we need."

"All right. She can stay for now." Arlo got up off the carpet and touched the green light. The blue hole disappeared. Then he glared at Nan. "But I'll be watching everything. The minute you do something stupid, I'm going to send you right back where you came from. This crisis is too important. It calls for heroes, not some little nobody."

Jerry knew he would've been tempted to teach the guy a lesson in manners if Arlo'd made a threat like that to him. But of course Nan had already made her point. No wonder those gang members had run when she came on the scene; maybe they could tell just from looking at her what a tough kid she was.

Serena put an arm around Jerry's shoulder. "I'm Doctor Serena Mep Cee, and this is Doctor Arlo Kam Pike. If you're feeling well enough now, we can all go into the next room and meet the other members of your team. Then we'll explain everything."

Walking together, Jerry saw the angry look in

Nan's dark eyes. He nudged her shoulder to encourage her.

"Some nobody!" he whispered.

She gave him a small grin and nudged him back. "Huh! Some hero!"

Side by side they stepped forward into the world of their future—a world that claimed to need them.

6

As they followed the people from the future into the room across the hall, Jerry puzzled over something that still didn't seem right. So far, he only had their word that this was the year 2345. Now that he was feeling better he started wondering. It could be a trick. These guys didn't seem like ordinary kidnappers, but how could he be sure? Maybe they'd taken him so his dad would reveal some secret physics stuff to them.

The tunnel had seemed weird enough to be future tech, but it could have been created by special effects, like in a movie. And if that was true, then Arti had lied, and he'd never see Rufus again. He was going to have to be on guard against tricks.

Out of the corner of his eye Jerry saw Nan putting out a hand and poking the walls when she thought no one was looking. Nan was suspicious of this place too. Once she ran a hand over the computer-dog's head as if she were looking for something that might prove it wasn't what it said it was.

Then he thought of something else. "Wait a minute."

The woman with the golden hair turned to Jerry. "What is it?"

Doctor Serena Mep Cee was beautiful enough to be a movie star, Jerry thought. It would be too bad if she turned out to be a criminal.

"Last year, my parents took me to see the Royal Shakespeare Company perform *Romeo and Juliet* in Los Angeles," he said. "It was a little hard to understand."

"Maybe you weren't paying attention!" Doctor Pike said.

"No, Arlo," Doctor Cee said. "I think I have an idea where this is going. Go on, Jerry."

Jerry continued, "From Shakespeare's time to mine is about four hundred years, but the English language has changed. So how come we can understand you perfectly if you're from more than three hundred years in the future? Wouldn't there be some differences? Some new words we couldn't understand, things like that?"

Doctor Cee smiled at him as if he'd just said something super intelligent. "You wouldn't have too many problems with our form of English, Jerry. A few new words have been added, but not too much has changed. But you might have difficulty with another member of the team. So we're going to give you nannies to take care of it."

"We're too old for babysitters!" Nan said grumpily.

"Not babysitters," Jerry guessed. "*Nannies*. I think it comes from 'nanotech.'"

"That's right. We inject a nanny for language under the skin of your upper arm, and it travels to your brain," Doctor Cee explained. "If we'd had real language differences in the team, we'd have given you a device called a broca amplifier instead. But this should be all you need."

Nan cut in. "I told you. I don't do drugs!"

Doctor Cee shook her head. "Nanotech has nothing at all to do with drugs."

It didn't sound to Jerry like the kind of explanation ordinary kidnappers would've thought up. Maybe these guys were for real. But he still wasn't one hundred percent convinced.

"This is wasting time!" Doctor Pike complained. "Let's go next door."

The next room was set up for conferences with a long polished wood table and six chairs. In the middle of the table was a thin glass plate. Two of the chairs were occupied. A fair-haired boy with very red cheeks who looked about twelve sat in one; next to him was a pretty girl about Jerry's own age with dark blue eyes and red curly hair cut short. They both wore sky blue jumpsuits.

"Jerry, Nan, meet Will Foxcroft and Ailee Wu Lovell, the other team members. Ailee's from our time," Doctor Cee said.

She touched the glass plate in the middle of the long table. Jerry could see the other kids' feet through it, but when her fingers made contact it clouded over then cleared again. He stared down into depth.

An Elizabethan galleon with sails billowing in the wind and flags flying moved through blue water. The sailing ship was so real he felt he could lean through the glass and touch it.

He was impressed. "That's a great hologram!"

Nan peered over his shoulder. "What's it supposed to be?"

"Sir Francis Drake's galleon, the *Golden Hind,* leaving what is now called California, on July twenty-third, 1579," Doctor Pike said. "But Captain Drake hasn't been knighted yet, and won't be till 1580 when the ship gets back to England from its round the world voyage."

"Bit small, wasn't it?" Nan commented. She still sounded grumpy. "How could anyone go around the world in that?"

"Seventy feet from stem to stern," Doctor Pike said. "It carried a crew of eighty men and boys."

"You could put four of them end to end on a football field!" Nan reached out to put a finger on what had been the plate glass surface. The finger kept on going right through the ship's main mast.

"Will's a cabin boy on the *Golden Hind*," Doctor Cee told them. "That's the day we yanked him."

Doctor Cee touched the table and the galleon disappeared. Jerry could see feet through the glass again. The short kid said something that Jerry vaguely recognized as Elizabethan English, but the accent wasn't at all like the one the actors had used in *Romeo and Juliet*, and he couldn't get the meaning.

Doctor Cee explained, "I'll get your nannies right away. Then you'll understand." She went over to a cabinet on one wall.

"You expect us to believe this stuff?" Nan asked. "Tricks and mumbo-jumbo explanations."

"If you don't like it here, you can always go back," Doctor Pike snapped.

Doctor Cee, who had her back turned to them, made a small, disapproving noise. "Arlo, please calm down."

Nan shook her head.

Doctor Cee came back with two small bottles on a tray. Nan shuddered. Jerry pushed his shirt sleeve up. He felt a tiny sting and turned to grin at Doctor Cee. Then it was Nan's turn. She scrunched her eyes up tight and looked as if she were holding her breath.

"Easy, Nan," Doctor Cee said.

Will Foxcroft said something to them, but again Jerry didn't quite understand it.

"How long will this take?" Jerry asked.

"About ten minutes," Doctor Cee said. "Sit down, and we'll start to explain Operation Hourglass to you while we wait."

Arti lay down at Doctor Cee's feet, a wise expression on his face.

"We have a very peaceful world," Doctor Pike began when they were all sitting at the conference table. "None of the wars and riots you have in your time. We've worked hard to get rid of even the idea of conflict. All disagreements are settled by discussion. We have space colonies, and we've thoroughly explored the solar system. There's no poverty anymore, no hunger, and just about every disease has a cure. Our world is perfect."

"At least, it was perfect, until a while ago," Doctor Cee added.

"Then, about fifteen years, ago several important things happened," Doctor Pike continued. "You don't need to know all the details. Just understand that a friendly race of superior aliens visited us. We call them the Gift Givers because they gave us the technology to travel almost instantly across the solar system and elsewhere in the galaxy, wherever there are teleportals set up. And we've developed a new twist on these 't-ports,' moving to the fourth dimension, Time. That's how we brought you here from the past."

"Traveling faster than the speed of light?" Jerry remembered his physics. "Einstein said FTL wasn't possible."

Doctor Pike said, "We're not talking about FTL,

just teleporting. Our spaceships don't go much faster than the ones of your time."

"Why did the Gift Givers give us this technology? What was their motive?" Jerry asked.

"We don't know. We have reason to believe we're being prepared for something, but they wouldn't tell us what," Doctor Cee said.

"Maybe it's a Trojan Horse," Jerry said. "You know, the people of Troy should've been suspicious of Greeks bearing gifts."

"The problem is," Doctor Cee explained, "we aren't the only young race that received teleportation from the Gift Givers. Others were given the technology at almost exactly the same time. We've had visitors on our colony worlds and space stations. And some of them aren't very nice at all."

"If you're as clever as you claim, why can't you do something about it?" Nan asked.

Doctor Cee and Doctor Pike looked at each other for a second. Jerry thought they seemed embarrassed.

Arti gave them the answer. "A century and a half of peace has made humans lose the art of fighting. They've spent so much time working for peace and safety they don't know how to deal with danger anymore."

"You mean you've forgotten how to fight." Nan sounded disgusted.

Jerry noticed that Doctor Cee looked uncomfortable at that. He did the math in his head. "Arti said 'a century and a half.' But if this is 2345—"

Doctor Cee glanced away. There was an awkward pause.

"Lot of things you aren't telling us," Nan said. "There's trouble coming in our time, isn't there? It's not going to be peaceful right away."

Jerry glanced at Nan. She was sharp as well as gutsy, he thought. She was going to make a good team member . . . whatever that meant.

"Not at first," Doctor Pike said, sounding as if this was something he didn't want to talk about right now.

"We need people from earlier times who still have the instinct to face unforeseen danger and overcome it," Doctor Cee explained. "As Arti says, people with 'grit.' "

Jerry felt a slight buzz like static electricity pass through him. He glanced at Nan, who was making a face as if she had indigestion. For a moment, his mouth felt dry. Then the feeling went away.

"What I don't understand is why you brought kids here instead of adults," Jerry said.

"Yeah," Nan added. "We've got plenty of generals and admirals in our time who could do the job for you."

Will, the boy from 1579, leaned forward grinning. "Only children can use the t-ports in safety," he said. "They be dangerous for anyone full grown."

Jerry found he understood every word Will spoke.

"What happens to the adults?" Nan wanted to know.

"It's not a pretty story," Doctor Cee said somberly. "We wouldn't use children if there were any other way. But now we can all discuss the mission we brought you here for. We'll explain everything. And then you can decide whether you want to help or not."

"**W**e want to send the three of you to Oort One," Doctor Pike said.

"Four," Arti corrected. The computer-dog winked at Nan.

Doctor Pike frowned. "Four, then. It's a small scientific base out on the edge of the solar system. They've been tracking comets. But now there's a serious problem. Ailee just got back from surveying the situation on Oort One. She'll tell you the details."

Nan looked at Ailee Wu Lovell. She guessed the red-haired girl was about her own age, or maybe a year older, like Jerry. But even that was young to be a scientist on a space station, wasn't it? If it was only the kids who could t-port because it was dangerous for adults, that changed everything. She could see how teenagers had become very important all of a sudden. Wouldn't the counselors at Oak House be amazed to know that! She was beginning to feel better about the future.

"Oort One is a small station on the edge of the Oort Cloud," Ailee began. "You know where that is, of course."

Nan didn't know where it was. Maybe she'd been

on suspension from school the day they discussed the Oort Cloud.

Jerry said quickly, "It's about forty thousand AUs distant from the sun. Astronomical Units mean the distance from the Earth to the sun. The Oort Cloud's where comets come from."

Nan nodded as if she'd known that all along. Jerry was a nice enough kid, but he showed off his knowledge of science in a way that was already getting on her nerves. She was going to have to put him in his place pretty soon.

Then she almost laughed out loud. Here she was, Miss Nobody yanked into the future by accident to do who knew what, and she was already preparing to take over and run the show! Grampa Hong would be proud.

"I knew naught of the Oort Cloud before I came here," Will explained. "Captain Drake makes use of an astrolabe to navigate by the stars, but even he knows not there be planets after Saturn."

"That's right," Jerry said. "Uranus wasn't discovered until William Herschel saw it in 1781. Neptune's discovery came in 1845. And tiny little Pluto had to wait till 1930 to be discovered."

What a showoff! Nan thought. But she noticed that Ailee was smiling at Jerry as if she were impressed. Nan deliberately ignored Jerry and turned to Will. "You'll have a lot to tell your captain when you get back, won't you?"

Then she realized that Doctor Cee and Doctor Pike were looking at her strangely. "What did I say?"

The computer-dog coughed politely. "Do you suppose it would be a good thing for Will, or any of you, to take back a lot of strange knowledge? People might start wondering."

Will grinned. "The gossips would say I commanded the powers of great witchcraft!"

"Oh, I get it," Nan said. "You're going to zap us with some kind of light so we forget everything, like in a science-fiction movie?"

Doctor Cee shook her head. "Not quite. Please go on, Ailee."

"Oort One's been doing comet research for a couple of years now," Ailee explained. "When we first got the t-ports from the Gift Givers, their gravitational influence disturbed comets in the Oort Cloud. You can imagine that even a small comet suddenly heading toward Earth could be a big problem."

"Like Shoemaker-Levy 9 that smacked into Jupiter a few years ago, our time," Jerry said. "That was a spectacular event."

"Yes. Your scientists learned a lot from it," Doctor Cee said. "And there've been more 'events' like that since your time."

Nan saw that if she didn't say something, Jerry and Doctor Cee would have a long, boring conversation about comets.

"You said there's a serious problem," she reminded them. "Get to the point."

"What a rude girl you are!" Doctor Pike spluttered.

But Arti shook his head so the long ears flapped. "I would remind you again, dear doctors, that excessive politeness may be one of our problems, a symptom of how we've lost the edge."

Ailee gazed at Nan. "You're right. We don't have time to waste. Oort One is being overrun with alien pests."

Ailee touched the glass in the middle of the conference table. This time a shaft of light sprang up above the surface and they all leaned forward to look.

Nan stared. She knew what a hologram was, of course; she just had never seen one as good as this. She recognized a working model of the solar system, a bit like one she'd seen on a fifth grade outing to Griffith Park Observatory in Los Angeles. That was the last time she remembered being happy in school.

Tiny jewel-colored worlds spun around the glowing sun, blue Earth, green Venus, red Mars, orange Jupiter. Between Mars and Jupiter, a twinkle of little lights marked the asteroid belt. And out at the very edge of the solar system where Ailee was pointing with a thin silver rod, Nan saw a misty swirl of cloud, home of the comets.

A lot of tiny black dots sprinkled the solar system. There were several dots on Earth itself, on the Moon, a few more in the asteroid belt. Three more were out at the edge of the solar system, and Ailee used the silver rod to point at one.

"What you're seeing here are deep space t-ports," Ailee said. "To get here, we basically jump first from Earth to the Moon, then to the t-port on Ceres in the asteroids, and then to Edge Station Two in the Cloud. That's what we call a sally port, the site for deep space jumps. A shuttle ferries us from Edge Two to Oort One, our space station."

Ailee's silver rod traced the journey to the space station.

"Will, you can think of a space station as a galleon in the middle of an ocean of sky," Doctor Cee said.

"And that shuttle be a shoreboat, rowing the crew to land?" Will asked.

"Yes, you could say that," Doctor Cee agreed.

"They're all kids running that space station, right?" Nan asked, checking.

"Unfortunately. Adults can't t-port that far," Doctor Pike said gloomily. "We have to go the slow, old-fashioned way by sleep-ship. And that takes years."

Jerry and Will peered into the sparkling model, but Nan was way ahead of them. She wanted to know what happened to adults if they tried t-porting. But right now there were other things on her mind.

"You said aliens can use the t-ports too," she said. "And I bet that's where they sneak into our solar system, right there at Edge Two."

Doctor Cee said, "You're absolutely right, Nan."

They were all looking at her as if she'd turned into a female Einstein.

"And now the aliens are on Oort One," Ailee added.

8

"**H**ow do these alien pests get from the sally port to our space station?" Nan asked.

In answer, Ailee touched the table top and the shining model of the solar system disappeared. In its place, Nan saw something that looked like a cross between a baby's ring of huge plastic beads and a construction toy her brother once had. In the center were four units shaped like long oil drums connected together by smaller round ones to a central corridor. Off at angles, she could see long thin scaffolding booms that framed the station and supported rows of radar dishes and radio antennae.

"Oort One," Ailee explained. She touched the four large cylinders in turn. "The Command Module, housing communications and control—Command for short. The Science and Research Laboratory Module, or SRL. Habitat, with the dorms and galley in it. And the Logistics and Utility Module, or LUM, where the power plant is."

Then the silver rod touched something in the hologram that looked like a tiny flying insect.

"That's the shuttle," Ailee said. "It ferries the team members between the station and the deep space terminal. And apparently the aliens have been stowing away in our luggage for the trip from Edge Station Two."

"These aliens can't be very big," Nan said.

"About the size of a little mammal called a gerbil, only round," Ailee said. "Gerbils aren't extinct in your time, are they? I can never remember which animals we've had to revive from their DNA."

Will looked puzzled.

"Think of them as furry rats," the computer-dog suggested.

"I used to have gerbils, before I got Rufus," Jerry commented. "They're cute little creatures."

"Remember these aren't gerbils. Just the same size," Doctor Cee warned.

"But how can something that small be a threat?" Nan asked. If the people of the future were scared of little animals, that was a very bad sign.

"One or two of them aren't a threat at all," Doctor Pike said. He was leaning back against the wall, his arms folded over his chest. "Ants make a better comparison than gerbils. Ants and bees are what we call 'hive mind' creatures. Individually, they're not very bright and hardly dangerous. But as soon as you have a lot of them you begin to see some effects. They can build an anthill or construct honeycombs. We think these aliens might be like that."

"We don't know the aliens' real name, what they'd call themselves if they were intelligent enough to use language, so we've given them one that we think fits," Doctor Cee said. "Thogemags."

"It's sort of a joke," Arti added.

Nan thought it was a dumb name, even if it was a joke. "What's the problem with the Thogs getting together?"

"In some way we don't understand, they disturb

41

electronic equipment," Doctor Cee explained. "In your time, I think a parallel would be to the interference you get on a television screen if somebody runs a hair dryer or a power saw nearby."

"You might as well give up watching," Jerry agreed.

The way Jerry seemed to accept everything they said so easily made Nan feel edgy. She wasn't so sure about these people.

"When ten or more of them get together," Ailee continued, "they can disrupt Oort One's lighting. Once they interfered with the Deep Space telescope."

"That's an inconvenience," Doctor Cee said. "But what if they accidentally disrupt the life support systems? A lot of kids would die."

"Accidentally?" Jerry queried.

"So far, we have no evidence that these 'Thogs,' as Nan called them, have much intelligence," Doctor Cee said.

The hologram faded away and the conference table became just an ordinary table again. Nan slid her fingers across the glass when nobody was looking. It felt just like regular glass.

"It shouldn't be too difficult to get rid of pests like that," Jerry said. "What have you tried?"

"That's the problem," Ailee said. "They seem so cute and cuddly that it's hard to get people to do anything to them. And they pull some kind of mental effect on us."

That sounded like an excuse to Nan. *Mental effect, huh? Gimme a break!* she thought. She wasn't as softhearted as these people from the future. "So the station kids aren't taking the danger seriously?"

Doctor Pike said, "Not seriously enough."

"Sometimes," Will said, "a captain hath no recourse but to abandon the sinking ship. Then he and his crew live to fight again another day.''

"We can't do that, Will,'' Doctor Cee said. "First, the work done at Oort One is far too important for us to abandon it, even temporarily. And secondly, if we don't stop these aliens here, then their next stop might be Earth itself.''

Doctor Pike added, "It's a source of great sorrow to adults that we can't t-port out there ourselves. It's distressing and unnatural to leave dangerous jobs like this to children.''

Everybody was silent for a moment after that.

"Well,'' Doctor Cee said. "That's the background. We'll teach you anything we think might help. Skills. Science. But basically we can't tell you any more about how to handle this crisis. I won't lie to you by saying there won't be any danger at all because we can't be certain.''

Doctor Cee paused for a moment and looked around the group, meeting each kid's eyes in turn. Nan felt a tingle run down her spine. Whatever doubts she had about these people, their danger was real. She did believe that.

"And now comes the moment for your decision,'' Doctor Cee said. "You have free choice. You've heard the facts. If you don't want to take the risk, we'll send you back to your own times right away. You can go on with your own lives undisturbed by this brief visit to your future.''

Nan spoke up first. "I'm staying!''

"Aye,'' Will said, nodding his head.

"Right!'' Jerry said. "When do we start?''

"Thank you,'' Doctor Cee said. "You don't know how much we appreciate your help. We'll send Arti along with you. But I have to tell you one thing about

AIs. Sometimes they seem to suffer from alien over-load.''

"What's that?'' Jerry asked.

"A heavy influx of new or very alien material can make them temporarily shut down,'' Doctor Pike said.

"I know how to start the Arti up again,'' Ailee said hastily.

Could be a recipe for disaster, Nan thought, if Arti shut down at the wrong moment. Better not to count on the computer-dog's help. But then she thought of something else. "What if you don't like the solution we come up with? You still going to support us?''

"I don't understand you,'' Doctor Pike said grumpily. He didn't seem able to keep up a pleasant mood for long.

Will laughed. "It be very like Captain Drake fighting Spaniards at sea. They be our enemies. I too have sent an enemy down five fathoms!''

Doctor Pike looked green when he heard that, but Nan figured Will was exaggerating. More likely he'd just wanted to, she thought. Then again, life was different in Francis Drake's day.

Jerry said, "You picked us because we weren't like you, remember?''

"That's why we brought you here,'' Doctor Cee agreed.

"Then you've got the right team,'' Nan said.

Doctor Cee set up a routine for them. In the mornings they studied the things she and Doctor Pike thought might help the team. That included space science, lessons in how to access all the information they might need through the Library unit of CenCom (the central computer that ran things), physics so they could begin to understand how the t-ports worked, and electronics for dealing with emergencies the aliens caused.

Jerry enjoyed the morning science sessions, but he noticed that Nan often had to struggle to keep up, and it seemed to go right over Will's head altogether. To the boy from 1579, this must all seem like magic. "Science" as Jerry knew it hadn't even been thought of in Will's time.

In the afternoons, Master Lobo worked with them on martial arts to sharpen their defensive reflexes. And sometimes they went on field trips.

"This afternoon we're going to the zoo," Doctor Pike said at the end of the first week of training.

"That be wondrous news!" Will said. Then he added, "What be a zoo?"

"A kind of park where they keep animals from

around the world," Nan said. "Tigers, elephants, stuff like that."

"Perchance Good Queen Bess hath beasts like that at Hampton Palace," Will said doubtfully. "But I have not been up to London."

"I thought you lived in England?" Nan said.

"Aye," Will said. "In Plymouth Port. A very long journey to London Town!"

"Remember, Nan," Doctor Pike said. "No trains and no freeways in Will's time. If he wants to go to London, he has to walk or ride a horse."

Jerry wasn't paying much attention to this discussion; he was mulling over a puzzle. He wouldn't have been surprised if Doctor Cee took them on a trip to a zoo because she was the kind one, but Doctor Pike didn't do nice things for them. He seemed to be just about the only grumpy person in this future, at least, the only one they'd met so far. Jerry suspected Pike had an ulterior motive.

"Let's get going," Doctor Pike said.

The flying car was waiting for them outside the Central Operations Building. Jerry thought the car looked just like a safari bus on a photo shoot in Africa, only with a plexiglass top instead of fringed canvas. Doctor Pike stopped to talk to another adult member of the project team. The kids waited in the shade of a large tree.

"How come we don't get to try out the t-ports?" Nan grumbled. "We're supposed to be training for this mission. So why don't we train with t-ports?"

Jerry knew he and Nan were going to have it out one of these days. Only room for one team leader, and he'd been brought here for the job. But her question was a fair one; he'd wondered about that too. Now they both looked to Ailee to hear the answer. He was glad Ailee was on the team; she was bright and pleasant, and she wasn't always arguing with him the way Nan was. She was pretty, too, but not in the stuck-up way of most of the girls in his school.

"It's because Doctor Pike's going with us," Ailee said.

"Is he chicken or what?" Nan demanded.

"All adults get headaches if they use the t-ports too often, even the ones for short jumps on Earth," Ailee explained. "Most people use old-fashioned methods of traveling for short trips like this one."

So flying cars, which were not even possible in his own time, were "old-fashioned" now in this future. The idea amused Jerry.

Doctor Pike came back and they climbed into the aircar. It was a beautiful day; the sun shone on the distant sapphire ocean, and the air was so clear Jerry could see snow-capped mountaintops hundreds of miles away.

"No air pollution. No water pollution. Everything in balance," Doctor Pike lectured them. "We've repaired all the mistakes of the past, healed all the wounds to nature, rebuilt all the beautiful monuments."

Jerry saw Nan rolling her eyes. But he had to admit, Doctor Pike seemed to be telling the truth about his world. Doctor Pike touched a button that made the top slide back out of the way so they could enjoy the mild breeze. They were heading for a range of low hills, swooping down into a narrow canyon between them.

The smell got to Jerry before he could actually see the zoo.

"Phew!" he said. "What's that?"

Nan was holding her nose too, but Will looked unconcerned. It probably got quite raunchy on those galleons after a few weeks, Jerry thought; the Elizabethans weren't hot on personal hygiene or doing the laundry regularly. Actually, this smell wasn't so bad, but it was different from any animal smell he remembered.

"You'll find out soon enough!" Doctor Pike said.

Jerry realized the trip to the zoo wasn't a treat for the team but a test of some kind. He wanted to warn the others to be on their guard, but couldn't see how to do that with Pike listening to everything.

The aircar landed in front of a long, low building with a red tile roof that reminded Jerry of the missions back in California, except this one was obviously nowhere near as old.

"I'll bet that's the gift shop," he said.

Pike nodded without saying anything.

"Some things never change," Jerry added for something to say while he figured out what was going on.

They headed toward an arch, and had to wait a minute while a group of little schoolkids in rainbow-colored uniforms went ahead. On the other side of the arch, they were in a lush, humid forest.

As the excited chattering of the schoolkids faded out ahead of them on the path, the air filled with loud squawks and roars and trumpetings. Jerry couldn't see any cages. So far, it didn't look much like a zoo. Doctor Pike didn't say anything, but Jerry noticed the scientist was watching the team when he thought they weren't paying attention to him.

Suddenly, something huge and bright green with claws and leathery wings came swooping out of a tree, heading straight for a pond. Then the thing changed its mind, veered away and disappeared back into the moss-hung trees.

Jerry whistled in surprise.

Will's face had turned gray. "Be that a dragon?"

"No such thing as dragons," Nan said firmly.

Doctor Pike stared at her. "Then tell us what it was, Nan Smith, if you're so sure."

Jerry knew it wasn't a good thing to put Nan on the spot here. Science of any kind wasn't her strong point. The team needed to stick together, one filling in for another.

"I believe it was a pterodactyl," he said. "But the ones I've seen illustrated weren't that bright emcrald color."

"Well, that's what hatched," Doctor Pike said grumpily. "Things don't always turn out as we expect."

Pike was talking about their team with that last comment, Jerry realized, not the flying creature. He was right; this visit to the zoo was some kind of test.

"One explanation of why humans all over the world have legends of dragons," Ailee said, "is that there's a kind of universal memory of dinosaurs."

"Monsters, mean you?" Will asked.

In Will's time people didn't know about dinosaurs. In his own case, Jerry didn't know how these scientists had produced a pterodactyl, but he did understand that it was scientifically possible. So before Doctor Pike could make Will feel bad, he spoke up.

"You bring back dinosaurs from fossil DNA?" he asked. "I never thought I'd actually see that for myself."

"We've got a lot of extinct animals here—" Ailee began.

Doctor Pike cut her off. "Take that path over there."

Pike headed off down the path, leading them. The man was obnoxious.

As Jerry made a move to follow, he caught sight of Nan, sticking her tongue out at Pike's back. Jerry chuckled.

10

They hadn't gone more than a few yards down the path when Nan saw another weird-looking creature in the bushes. This one had short stubby legs, a scaly ridge along its back, a nasty-looking horn on its snout, and a very bad attitude.

She could tell Will was nervous because he didn't understand, and she knew that renaming his "monsters" as dinosaurs didn't help much.

She glanced at Doctor Pike and found him watching Will carefully, as if he were hoping to catch the boy doing something wrong. It almost seemed as if Pike was putting the team to the test, to see how smart they were or something.

She put a hand on Will's arm; she needed some distance between herself and Pike until she figured things out. The others went on down the winding path.

Will had been telling her about his life aboard a galleon in Drake's fleet. She couldn't see yet why they'd picked a kid from the sixteenth century for this mission. He didn't understand anything about technology. He didn't understand dinosaurs. How was he going to deal with aliens? What skill could he possibly have that they needed? *Grit,* they'd called it. But what did that mean?

"Tell me more about yourself, Will," she said. Will seemed happy enough to talk about himself. One thing about him she'd noticed already: he was a very sunny person. "Do you want to spend all your life at sea?"

"Aye. If God allows, some day I shall be page to Captain Drake," Will said.

"What does a page do?" she asked.

"I would stand behind my captain's chair when he sups and pour his wine," Will explained.

It didn't sound very exciting, but she could see Will liked the idea. "What's stopping you?"

"He hath a page, his cousin, a lad of fifteen years," Will said. "But soon enough John Drake shall be too old, and perchance I shall be chosen in his place."

"Life on your English ships sounds rough to me," she said. "But good luck with the page thing."

He grinned at her. "Think on it, Nan. To encompass the globe, that be a grand venture. But fighting the Spaniard and taking his gold be the best part!"

"In my time you wouldn't be old enough to fight," she observed.

"Old enough lies in the heart, and my heart serves my captain," Will replied seriously.

He was a tough kid, even if he did believe in magic and monsters. She didn't want to see Pike make a fool out of him.

Ahead of them on the path, the others had stopped to let them catch up. Doctor Pike looked furious that they'd lagged behind. What a jerk!

"Look, Nan," Jerry said. He pointed at a pair of large, clumsy-looking birds on the path ahead of them. "Dodos."

Nan laughed. Her roomie, Connie, had called the

House Mother a dodo once; she could see the resemblance to Mrs. Turner.

She started to feel better after that. It was a nice day, they were out of the classroom, and there were interesting extinct animals to look at. Here and there along the path there were weird plants that were extinct too, and some of the brightest-colored flowers on them smelled the sourest. She thought it was just as well they didn't grow in gardens anymore.

A little farther along, Ailee stopped. "Wait. This is my favorite."

They stood by an information sign on the path and stared into the jungle. Huge olive-green ferns shaded ponds full of tall reeds. Bright-colored birds flew among the branches of trees with thick, black trunks. But Nan saw no more pterodactyls. Then after a moment, they heard a low, rumbling growl. Something moved stealthily in the undergrowth.

Something very large.

The ferns parted and an enormous beast came out and stood gazing at them, twenty feet away. It was bigger than the biggest lion Nan had seen, with a huge, powerful head and terrifying, long daggerlike teeth in its upper jaw.

"What be this monster?" Will whispered.

"Saber-toothed tiger," Nan said softly. "What a beauty!"

"Ugh!" Will said. "Observe those teeth!"

"Actually," Jerry said, "its proper name is saber-toothed cat. It's not closely related to modern tigers at all."

"Same difference," Nan said firmly.

She knew she couldn't put off taking Jerry down a peg or two much longer. But right now her attention was on the tiger, because Will was right: It might be beautiful, but it was obviously dangerous, and it could decide to charge them. There was no fence in the way to save them if it did.

"*Smilodon californicus,*" Pike said. "Like everything here, they're extinct in your time. Probably just as well."

"I like not the look of this beast," Will whispered to Nan.

As if it picked up their fear, the beast suddenly snarled, bared its fangs, lowered its head and rushed toward them! Horrified, Nan saw the glistening sharp dagger teeth.

Jerry grabbed Will, who was nearest to him, and shoved him off the path in a hurry.

An icy fear washed over Nan too, but something didn't make sense. If there was real danger here, surely Doctor Pike wouldn't have risked all their lives? Hers, maybe, but not Jerry's and Ailee's and Will's. She decided to stand her ground.

At the last second, the beast turned away from them, muscles rippling, then stood still under the trees.

Nan's heart was thumping so hard it hurt.

"What's this, Nan Smith?" Pike demanded. "Another example of your foolish courage?"

So that was it. He wasn't testing all of them. Just her. Pike hadn't liked her from the first minute. She knew he'd be delighted to find a reason to get rid of her. He was waiting for her to make a mistake. She stared hard at the man. She hadn't paid much attention to science classes at school. But she'd taken her brother Ti to all the *Star Trek* and *Star Wars* movies, and that gave her an idea.

"It's a force field," she said. "The animals here are surrounded by an invisible barrier that prevents them from getting out and harming people. That's why there are no cages."

Doctor Pike actually looked disappointed. She laughed out loud. She'd guessed right.

"Way to go, Nan!" Jerry said. He turned to Will. "I'll explain it to you later."

"Don't let it go to your head," Pike said to Nan. "Overconfidence will be as dangerous as ignorance on this mission. Don't get conceited."

"We have a pair of smilodons," Ailee broke in. "We found the DNA for them in skeletons trapped in the La Brea Tar Pits in Los Angeles. They're carnivores. They lived in the Pleistocene from about 1.6 million years ago until about eight thousand years ago. They were great hunters, but when their prey got stuck in the tarry pools where they'd come to drink, so did the hungry smilodons."

"I would sooner face the Spaniard than this monster," Will said. He still looked pale.

The others started back along the path, taking a short cut to the exit, but Nan lingered. She'd managed to pass this test Pike had arranged for her; she hoped she'd be as lucky with any others he planned. He didn't seem to like any of the kids very much, but she was obviously the main target for his anger.

Turning to follow them, she saw the sign giving information about the tigers:

The adult Smilodon *is about two-thirds as long as the Bengal Tiger (see exhibit 15). It uses its large upper canine teeth to inflict fatal wounds on its prey. Its jaws can open 120 degrees, twice as wide as a modern cat. Like modern cats, it possesses intact hyoid bones which allow it to purr, but unlike tigers, whose hyoid bones fail to develop, the smilodon does not roar. Like both, it is a ferocious hunter.*

She glanced at the smilodon still standing just a few feet away on the other side of the invisible force field barrier. It was a female. In spite of the eight-inch nightmare daggers that extended below the animal's chin now that her jaw was closed, she was a magnificent creature. The liquid amber eyes that gazed at Nan reminded her of the Oak House cat. She'd always been fond of felines. This one had a round soft belly, and she knew enough about cats to tell the smilodon was going to have a cub.

"I'm not afraid of you," she said. "Even if you could eat our little Tiger in one gulp."

The smilodon yawned at that, revealing other sharp teeth in her jaws as well as the sabers for which she was named. Then she moved lazily away, graceful in spite of her huge size.

Nan ran to catch up with the others, who were almost back to the gift shop by now. When she got there, Doctor Pike held up his hand for silence.

"I admit I'm surprised," he said. "But you all did well on the tests you faced today. Even you, Nan Smith."

She shrugged as if it were no big deal. She wasn't about to let him know she'd been worried for even a second.

Doctor Pike gave one of his rare, cold smiles. "But don't relax just yet. I'm going to be watching carefully."

11

"**T**-porting is obviously dangerous," Jerry said.

He, Nan, and Will were sitting on the marble steps of the Central Operations Building's front door the day after the zoo trip, waiting for their escort to take them on their first t-port experience. Usually in the afternoon they were scheduled for an hour of practice with Lobo, their martial arts master. But Master Lobo had gone to judge a competition in China. Today they were going to leave the city of Kern, where the operation was housed, and jump over to China for a visit.

Neither Arlo Pike nor Serena Cee was going with them. Jerry was happy not to have Pike along, especially after the sneaky test he'd arranged for them at the zoo, but he'd noticed before that Serena didn't t-port either unless she absolutely had to.

"That's what I figure too," Nan said. "But why is it more dangerous for adults than for kids?"

"We be superior!" Will punched a fist in the air.

Jerry glanced at him. Will was learning too many future mannerisms; they'd get him in trouble when he went back to 1579.

"What's different about us as kids?" Jerry said, thinking aloud. "What changes or stops when we're fully grown?"

Nan said, "Maybe that's it. We haven't finished growing."

"I thought of that," Jerry said. "It could be a function of mass. The more a person weighs, the more hazardous the trip through the time or space dilation of a t-port."

"Then why do they not send small adults?" Will asked.

"You're right," Jerry agreed. "It can't have to do with weight."

"Could it have something to do with our brains?" Nan asked.

"I'll have to think about it some more," Jerry said.

Doctor Cee had told them that when the Gift Givers first gave humans the t-ports in deep space, people rushed to take ships through. But that had turned out to be a horrible mistake because the adults on board either died or had their brains turn to mush. Even jumping within the solar system held very big risks for adults. Only the kids survived unhurt. With friends like the Gift Givers, Jerry thought, people didn't need enemies.

"You know something?" Nan said. "If t-porting affects aliens the same way, then maybe those gerbil-creatures, the Thogs, are juveniles too."

Before they could discuss it, Ailee came out of the building with Arti. Jerry still found it weird to see how the AI resembled his dog, Rufus, except for the steely eyes like camera lenses.

"Since I'll be your companion on the trip out to Oort One," Arti said, "I'm going to accompany you today too."

Ailee led them across the street to a small glass-sided hut that Jerry had figured was a news vendor's shack. When she opened the door, he saw he'd been mistaken. As soon as they were all inside—a tight fit—Ailee touched a code into a pad on the wall.

The back wall suddenly disappeared.

"Come along," Ailee said, stepping into a gray mist.

He followed her into the mist, but Will hung back.

"Come on, Will," Nan said. "Just hang on to my hand and pretend it's a ride at Disneyland."

No such thing as Disneyland in Will's century, Jerry thought as he stepped out the other side into an identical booth. But then, how would you explain this sort of thing to an Elizabethan? Nan and a reluctant Will came through after him just as Ailee was opening the door to the outside.

"Welcome to China," Ailee said.

"Xian, to be exact," Arti said. "A small city on one end of what used to be the fabulous Silk Road of the Middle Ages."

Jerry noticed that Nan was running her hands over her arms and legs. "What're you doing?"

"Reality check," she said gruffly. "Just making sure all of me got through in one piece."

Across the street there was a red-painted gate in a stone wall. Ailee led them through it into the cobblestone courtyard behind. A large temple with a tiled roof stood there, every inch painted and decorated in red and gold with Chinese ideograms and carved dragons and phoenix birds. Inside, the walls and the ceiling beams were as brightly decorated as the outside.

"This is fabulous!" Jerry gazed at the doorway. "Imagine how old this place must be. It was probably built a thousand years ago."

"No," Ailee said. "It's only about fifty. We rebuilt

it just like the thousand-year-old one that used to stand here.''

''Rebuilt? What happened to the original?''

To his surprise, Ailee turned red and looked away. The computer-dog coughed politely and Jerry glanced down at it.

''Shall we go in, my dear friends?'' Arti asked.

''Why don't you tell us about the temple?'' Nan demanded. ''What's the big deal?''

''Yes,'' Jerry said. ''It's about time you leveled with us.''

''No big deal, just a boring history lesson,'' Arti said soothingly, leading the way into the temple.

As they went in, Nan leaned toward Jerry and spoke in a low voice. ''They're hiding something. I think something really bad's going to happen between our time and this.''

''I think so too,'' he whispered back. ''But everything's obviously going to turn out okay in the end, or they wouldn't be here today, and they wouldn't have such a great world.''

''Maybe,'' Nan said, sounding reluctant.

In the middle of the cleared space, Master Lobo stood watching two boys who were trying to land kicks on each other. All around the temple, other boys and girls were performing set motions or sparring, with adult judges looking on and keeping score. It was quiet in here, everyone concentrating silently on the competition, except for the ritual shouts of ''Haiyah!'' coming from time to time from the contestants.

Ailee went over to tell Master Lobo they were here, and Will went with her. Arti lay down in a corner; it looked as if he'd gone to sleep, but Jerry saw one ear cocked to listen.

''They should've held this at the Shaolin Monastery, where kung fu started," Nan grumbled. "You might've seen some better form there. This is really terrible."

"Keep your voice down!" Jerry warned.

Too late. One of the guys nearby who'd just broken a board with the side of his hand glanced up and frowned. He seemed about Jerry's age and had a black belt knotted over a white tunic.

"Well, look who we have here," the guy announced. "The great Gerald Vanderburg and his little band of time travelers."

Several of the other young contestants stopped what they were doing to look. Most of them seemed uncomfortable with the guy's rude words.

Nan scowled. "What of it?"

"Who needs you?" the guy asked, brushing dark hair back out of his eyes.

"Zeb, please don't offend our guests," another boy said, taking the rude one's arm.

The muscular guy pushed the other boy off and came towards Jerry. "We're all highly trained in martial arts. And we grow up without the filth and disease that left you all such runts back in the Dark Ages!"

The guy had aimed that last remark at Will, but Drake's cabin boy just grinned confidently. It was Jerry who winced when the rude guy mentioned disease.

"Any one of us here could do the job!" the belligerent guy went on. "We don't need kids from the past."

"Look—Zeb, is it?" Jerry began, trying to keep the peace.

"You'll be sorry," Nan warned the guy, taking a step closer to Jerry.

Zeb ignored Nan and put up his hands as if he were

going to spar with Jerry. "I challenge you, Vanderburg. Show me your superior ability."

Jerry had no intention of fighting—it wasn't something he was any good at—but he was fascinated. It looked as if the guy were performing some kind of intricate ballet about fighting, his arms weaving in front of his face, his expression angry and intense as he performed the ritual movements warming up for a strike. Out of the corner of his eye, Jerry was aware of Master Lobo striding across the room toward them.

But before the master got there, Zeb suddenly fell on the floor. It didn't look as if Nan had moved, but of course she had. Remembering how she'd dumped Arlo Pike too, Jerry thought that anybody who challenged Nan had better be a black belt in more than one martial art.

"Nan! Jerry! What's going on?" Master Lobo asked.

Nan scowled at the guy on the floor. "My Chinese grandfather taught me: Don't boast, just act."

Then another group of kids came rushing over. They seemed more like what Jerry was used to finding here, polite and friendly.

"Please accept our apologies for Zeb's rudeness," a young dark-skinned boy said. "And be assured that we welcome you here."

A very pretty blonde girl said, "Did I hear Zeb say this is Gerald Vanderburg? Oh, let me shake your hand!"

She grabbed his hand and pumped it eagerly. Jerry felt his cheeks suddenly getting warm.

"I'm so honored to meet you," the girl said. "I've read about all the wonderful things you did—I mean, are going to do—that is—" She broke off suddenly.

She looked as embarrassed as Ailee had a few

minutes ago when they'd been asking about the re-built temple.

"Okay, let's break up the fan club," Master Lobo said, smiling. "I want to show our guests around."

The guy Nan had dumped got up slowly and held out his hand too, with a bit less excitement, Jerry noted.

"Good to meet you, Vanderburg," he mumbled. "No hard feelings."

"Right, Zeb," he agreed. "No hard feelings."

They stayed another hour, watching the competition and looking around the rebuilt temple as Master Lobo explained things.

"You can see we've kept up the martial arts," Master Lobo said. "Kung fu, karate, tae kwon doh, aikido. We just haven't had to use them for real in a very long time. We've lost the edge. That's why we need you."

Then it was time to go back to the project. Master Lobo handed them over to Arti again.

"See you on the morrow, my Master," Will said. "I am afire with impatience for my next lesson! Nobody on the *Hind* knows this skill of karate. The next time some knave takes thought to bully me . . ." He put his hands up in a warding-off stance to show what he intended to do to bullies.

"Not tomorrow," Master Lobo said. "Arti will explain."

Arti led the little procession out of the temple and over to the t-port booth.

"How can they love us and hate us for the same thing, being who we are?" Jerry asked.

"Hate's much too strong a word," Arti said. "But, yes, a few people do resent your presence here because it reminds them that their paradise has flaws they can't seem to fix without help. But the vast majority of our citizens are grateful for your help."

"Maybe they should talk some sense into the rest," Nan suggested sourly. "Get their acts together!"

Arti glanced at her. "It's a very minor problem."

Jerry could see the computer-dog was miffed by Nan's criticism. He decided to change the subject. "What am I going to do in the twenty-first century that they think is so wonderful?"

"Concentrate on the mission right now," Arti advised.

Nan asked, "Why won't we get our usual lesson from Master Lobo tomorrow?"

"The situation on Oort One has worsened," Arti said. "Our mission's been moved up. We leave tomorrow."

12

Nan woke before daylight. The trip to China the day before had reminded her of what Grampa had told her when she visited him in the convalescent home. The *I Ching* had promised success if she persevered.

"I'm going to persevere, Grampa," she said softly in the dark room. "You're going to be proud of me."

In the next bed, Ailee muttered in her sleep.

Nan thought about the team for a minute. Jerry was a brain; they'd be glad of his knowledge of science in the days to come. But he hesitated when she knew there were times you had to decide and act in a flash. Ailee knew the space station, but she didn't seem tough enough to stand up to enemies. Look at the remark she'd made about the gerbil-creatures being hard to deal with because they were cute! And Will was crafty, with good combat reflexes, but he was the youngest and without any science knowledge beyond knowing the Earth was round.

That meant only one thing. Nan Smith, the "nobody" they hadn't meant to yank out of the past, was going to have to lead the team.

"Are you awake?" Ailee's voice said.

"Yeah."

"I thought I heard the boys up next door." Ailee

sat up and touched the dark window. When she did, the glass became transparent and light streamed in.

Nan stared out at gardens that had become so familiar. Dew-covered grass and flowers twinkled in the rising sun; birds flashed through the trees singing their morning songs. Earth was a beautiful planet. If things went wrong, this might be the last time she saw it.

Nothing's going to go wrong! she told herself firmly.

Ailee headed for the shower. Nan grabbed shampoo and followed. Afterward, she dressed in a clean blue jumpsuit with the operation logo on it, an hourglass. She pulled her long black hair into one French braid. At the last minute, she remembered something. She turned back to the table beside her bed and picked up the flashlight from Ti.

Arti was waiting for them outside the same t-port booth they'd used yesterday; the computer-dog's fur shone red-gold in the sunlight. Doctor Pike stood with the AI, frowning as usual. Two other members of the staff who'd trained them stood with him, Doctors Chen and Orgel.

Doctor Cee came hurrying out of the building a moment later. "Jerry, Nan, Will," she said. "I'll ask you again. Are you sure you want to do this? There's no shame in changing your mind."

All three of them shook their heads.

"We're going to do the job," Jerry said.

Now that the moment had come at last, everybody stood around not knowing what to say. Nan glanced at the team. Everybody seemed excited except Will, who seemed nervous. This had to be hard on a kid from the sixteenth century.

"Well," Ailee said at last, opening the door to the booth. "Let's get going."

Then everybody talked at once.

"Take care of yourselves," Doctor Cee said.

Doctor Orgel said, "Wish I were going with you."

"Remember to check in with CenCom at regular intervals," Doctor Chen advised.

"Try not to do anything stupid!" That was Arlo Pike, glaring at Nan.

She wanted to stick her tongue out at him, but this politeness thing seemed to be getting to her too, so she settled for giving him a dark look.

Once again, Nan, Jerry, Ailee, Will, and Arti crowded into the little booth and Ailee touched the keypad. The wall dissolved and they walked through mist to find themselves in another booth.

"T-port at LEO One," Ailee said. "Come on."

Low Earth Orbit, Nan remembered the lecture. Her heart was beating faster with excitement. Next stop was a t-port behind the Moon, and then came a really big jump out to the asteroids. She'd asked why they couldn't just jump straight from Earth to the Oort Cloud, but she hadn't understood the answer. Jerry probably had.

Already the wall on the far side of this base was dissolving and Jerry and Ailee were going through. Will lagged behind, so she grabbed his hand and pulled him through with her. Hurrying after the others, she felt a slight tingle of energy running over her skin. She entered another t-port booth just in time to see the other two walking through yet another wall of fog.

"Now we're at the t-port on Ceres," Ailee said when they were all on the other side of the fog.

"We're in the Asteroid Belt. One more jump to the Cloud."

Nan wished she could stop for a moment and look out, if there'd been any windows. What would the asteroids look like? She imagined thousands of enormous potato-shaped rocks whizzing past, and then she was glad she couldn't see them after all.

A slight sound made her turn around. Will's face had gone completely white as if he were about to throw up.

"You okay?" she asked.

He managed a tiny nod but didn't say anything; he looked terrified.

"I can't explain how we're doing this, but it's not witchcraft," she said. "And it's not dangerous." *Keep your fingers crossed when you say that!* she thought. "I trust these people. You can too."

"Aye," Will said in a small voice. "It be like trusting the captain to bring us safe around the globe, though no Englishman hath done that before."

"Exactly," she said. "Just close your eyes and hold my hand."

Then she noticed he was clutching something tightly at his belt. "What have you brought?"

Will said, "I venture not into danger without the protection of my knife."

She glanced at the long-bladed knife he showed her. "You brought that with you through the time tunnel?"

Will nodded and tucked the knife inside his jumpsuit. "There be enemies everywhere."

She smiled. "You won't find any Spaniards where we're going."

They walked through the next misty wall. Her legs were starting to feel a bit rubbery. For a second she had the weird feeling that somehow her mind got there before her body, but of course that was nonsense. Spatial effects could be very strange, Serena Cee had warned them. At least they were nowhere near as bad as the temporal effects of the time tunnel.

"Edge Two sally port," Ailee announced. "This isn't the original one the Gift Givers provided. We've built this and all the t-ports on Earth in just fifteen years."

This time when they emerged from the booth they were in a wide hall. Alcoves opened off to small offices on three sides, and Nan saw terminals and banks of dials and gauges whose purpose she couldn't guess. The walls and floors had been painted bright colors to make up for a sun that was only pinprick size seen from this far out. The air in here was odd too, cool and fresh but not smelling of anything at all, unlike air on a real planet.

Teenagers and robots were hurrying back and forth, some carrying palm-size computers. E-pads, Ailee said they were called, electronic notepads. The kids wore some of the wildest, most colorful clothes Nan had seen outside of a Mardi Gras parade, no two dressed alike; but she understood the clothing, like the bright walls, was a deliberate contrast to the darkness of space. Most of the 'bots looked like kindergartners had constructed them out of tin cans and building blocks and wheels off some kid's wagon.

"I'm surprised there are so many people here," Jerry said.

"Think of this as a gateway," Ailee advised. "Remember what the history books say about the Middle Ages? Cities had walls to keep out robbers and invaders. Same thing here. Sometimes undesirable beings try to come through the gate. We have to have a way to keep the bad aliens out.''

Nan saw with surprise that a few people here were adults. "I thought adults couldn't t-port this far without risking getting hurt?''

"They came up here as teens,'' Ailee explained. ''Then they decided to stay because they thought their work was so important. Now they're too old to t-port home. They've dedicated their lives to keeping Edge Station Two and the other two sally ports operating safely. When they do go home again, they'll go the slow way, by cold-sleep ships.''

Even here on Edge Two, Ailee didn't let the team slow down. She led them at a fast pace down a corridor to the shuttle dock. "Don't set your backpacks down, and don't pick up anything,'' she warned. ''We don't want to gather any more Thogs while we're here.''

Nan glanced around but didn't see any of the furry aliens.

The waiting craft didn't look much like the shuttles that were launched from rockets in her day. What it did look like was a silver slug with a slightly pointed nose.

Ailee hurried them all aboard and into deep bucket seats, then checked their safety webbing. They were the only passengers. There was no pilot, for the shuttle was controlled by computer.

It took off silently; the only clue they had was a sensation of being shoved back in their seats by the acceleration. Jerry and Will peered out the shuttle's forward window, but Nan felt sleepy. She closed her eyes for just a moment.

"Nan! Wake up!" Will's voice said. "We have reached our galleon in the ocean of sky."

"You slept for almost two hours," Ailee said. "Welcome to Oort One, space station."

13

As soon as Jerry stepped through the airlock onto the space station, he spotted his first Thog rolling past. It was about the size of a tennis ball and covered in gray fur. There was nothing to show what was front or back or up or down. It had no feet or tail, and no face that he could see. It didn't look too scary.

The shuttle had docked at the airlock at the end of the central corridor nearest Oort One's command module. The team went through a transfer node into the module itself. The walls sloped gently up around him as if he were standing inside a giant soup can. He'd expected to find himself floating in zero gravity, but the station rotated to make artificial gravity. He felt lighter than he did on Earth, as if he'd lost a lot of weight, but he didn't go bouncing off every time he took a step.

The space station was a lot bigger than he'd imagined it was going to be. The two-thirds-size mockup they'd used to practice in had made him expect to feel crowded. He wouldn't get lost on Oort One, but at least he wouldn't be constantly bumping everybody's elbows. *Dad would love to see this!* he thought. His father was a great booster of the space program. Now he'd end up knowing far more than his dad had ever dreamed.

Ailee was greeting the kids on the station and introducing them to Nan and Will. Jerry figured they were mostly about his or Nan's age, but some seemed to be as young as twelve. He saw some robots trundling about. They weren't as cool as Arti; these 'bots resembled his mom's canister vacuum cleaner.

He stood over by a curving wall, hands in pockets. "You're not shy, are you?" Arti asked quietly.

"No, that's not it," he said.

But now that he was actually here, he was struck by the strangeness of seeing a functioning space station with not an adult in sight. It brought home to him the real problem with the technology the Gift Givers had presented to Earth. A few days before they'd left, Doctor Orgel had told him of some lost colonies from the early days before t-porting was fully understood. They were far outside the solar system, Doctor Orgel said, where no adults could go and where the original kid settlers were now adults themselves and couldn't come back.

Who were those mysterious Gift Givers, and why did they offer their gifts? He had a feeling that even if his team managed to solve the problem of the Thogemags, there would still be a lot of stuff left to do in 2345.

"Jerry!" Ailee grabbed his arm and pulled him over to meet a boy about his own age. "This is DeShawn Sig Gan, head of the astronomy team. You're going to bunk with him."

DeShawn had a dark brown face and a big, friendly smile that reminded Jerry of his friend Jim. He knew right away he was going to get on okay with DeShawn.

"Hey, dude!" Jerry said.

He saw Nan make a face at his choice of words. It wasn't what he'd usually say, but Arti had been partly right and he was feeling a bit awkward. Luckily, no one else seemed to notice.

After everyone had shaken hands, Ailee told the station kids to get back to work. Tracking comets was a deadly serious business since so many of them had been bumped from their safe orbits when the Gift Givers arrived with the sally ports. Many of the comets that were dislodged fell near Earth and the civilized parts of the solar system. They had to be tracked and sometimes stopped before they hit someplace where people lived.

The team took their personal stuff to the sleeping quarters they'd been assigned in the Habitat module. They were all told to meet in the galley for lunch. Since none of the team had eaten much at breakfast, nobody argued.

"It's weird not seeing any adults," Jerry said, as DeShawn led him through the sliding doors of the transfer node and down the narrow corridor that connected the command module with Habitat.

"Oh, we do get adults now and again from Edge Two," DeShawn said. "I guess our work here monitoring comets doesn't seem as exciting as keeping unwanted aliens out of the solar system, so they don't stay."

"In my time, nobody would dream kids could run a space station," Jerry commented.

"Things have been pretty bad here lately," De-Shawn admitted as they reached his cabin in the Habitat module. "While Ailee was gone, there was a terrible accident."

"Caused by the Thogs?" he guessed.

DeShawn looked thoughtful. "Possibly. We can't be certain. A kid was about to go outside the station on a routine check for damage to the aluminum skin of the science module from comet debris. That's a constant problem here in the Oort Cloud. He was in the airlock, waiting for the pressure to drop so he could step outside safely into vacuum. But something happened, and the outer doors opened too soon. He got swept out into space."

Jerry stared at DeShawn. "You don't mean—"

"Yeah," DeShawn said gruffly. "Nothing we could do."

Jerry shook his head. That was a terrible story.

His bunk was the top one, but it was easy to lob his duffel bag up there in this low gravity. Then they headed for the galley, which was on a lower deck of Habitat. A colorful holographic mural of the Rocky Mountains at sunset covered one wall and made up for the lack of windows. The chairs and long dining table were made of some plastic-looking material in primary colors, and they looked comfortably homey.

He missed having a window somewhere. Doctor Orgel had explained to them that solid walls were safer in an area constantly bombarded with comet debris. But he'd been looking forward to seeing the stars without the disturbance of Earth's atmosphere that made them seem to twinkle. The little glimpse he'd got from the shuttle left him hungry for more.

Nan, Ailee, and Will were there ahead of him, busy eating. Jerry took a seat opposite Will and stared in amazement at the younger boy's full plate.

"Ice cream, Jello, chocolate cake, jelly beans? What kind of lunch is that?" he asked.

"The best!" Will said, spearing up a chunk of cake with a long-bladed knife.

He'd noticed before that Will seemed to do a lot of his eating with this knife. Forks were apparently not used much at table on the *Golden Hind*.

"You need vegetables for vitamins," Jerry said. He wondered whether they knew anything about vitamins in Drake's day. "You know, to keep you healthy."

Will stood up, went over to a box on the wall that looked like a fancy microwave oven, and slowly spelled out a word on the control pad. In a second, two halves of a lemon appeared.

"My captain gives us these to prevent scurvy," Will said. He took half a lemon and squeezed the juice straight into his mouth. Then he made a face, set the lemon down, and went back to eating dessert.

Jerry saw that if there were no adults here to supervise, he might have to pretend to be one from time to time, if only to make sure that his team ate nutritious meals and kept their strength up. But right now was probably not the time to start. As soon as they finished eating, he'd call the first strategy meeting, and that might be one of the things he should mention.

"The food synthesizer can make almost anything," DeShawn said. He pointed to the box on the wall that Will had used.

Jerry chose pepperoni and mushroom pizza, and DeShawn typed his order in. At least it had meat, veggies and dairy products, but he realized it didn't set the good example he'd intended. He'd have to do better next time. He took a mouthful of pizza; it was hot and gooey, almost as good as his favorite pizza place back in Santa Marta. These future folks had it together when it came to the simple pleasures of life, he thought.

"So," Nan said pushing her empty soup bowl away. "Here's what we're going to do first."

Before he could object to the way she was trying to take over the team, the lights in the galley dimmed.

"Thogs," DeShawn said.

Will stood up and looked around. "Where be they?"

"Not necessarily in here," Ailee said, as the lights came back up again. "They could be anywhere. They hide in the walls, the heating ducts, everywhere."

"Better in there than out in the open," DeShawn explained. "When they have enough space, they curl around each other in a big, furry ball. That's when they seem to be able to do damage."

Then the lights went out altogether. A second later, an emergency system took over and lit the smaller, back-up lights along the walls. Jerry lost his appetite. He was suddenly aware of how vulnerable they were, on an isolated space station way out past the planet Pluto at the edge of the solar system, a station infested with pests that could put the lights out.

DeShawn said, "The trick is to keep them from ganging up on us. A dozen cause small equipment failures. More than twenty? We're afraid to find out."

Jerry wanted to say something reassuring like, "Don't be afraid. We're here now." But after the horror story DeShawn had told him about the accident, it sounded stupid, like something out of a bad sci-fi movie. So he said nothing.

In the low emergency lighting, the group found their way through the transfer nodule to the corridor leading back to the command module that housed the control center of the station. This module was brightly lit; Command hadn't been affected this time. Arti was waiting for them there.

Nan sat down in a chair in front of a bank of display panels. "One thing I learned in the mockup was that we can call up a diagram of the entire station," she said. "We ought to be able to see where either people or Thogs are hanging out."

Jerry felt irritated that she'd taken over. The chain of command would have to be settled between them. But at that moment a screen in front of Nan lit with a three-dimensional display of Oort One's building plans. He could tell it was a real-time display because little blue dots representing people moved along the corridors and catwalks of the station.

"How shall we know our enemy in that?" Will asked.

DeShawn leaned over Nan's shoulder and touched another button; the blue dots disappeared.

"Single Thogs don't show up for some reason," DeShawn explained. "Even couples are hard to see. But four or more in a ball show up red. Usually we don't have to wait to see them to know they're there. Something will have gone wrong with the station first."

No red dots appeared on the screen.

"We're safe for a while," Ailee said. "But we have to keep watch constantly for damage caused by the Thogs."

Then the screens blipped out and every light in the control center went out, including the emergency system.

In the darkness, Will's voice complained, "Fie! Even on the *Hind* we have candles."

14

"**I**'ve got something better than candles," Nan said. "A flashlight."

She dug the small light Ti had given her out of a pocket of her jumpsuit and turned on the beam. The flashlight sent a tiny circle of light onto the control panels and the blank screens. She moved it to illuminate the floor at their feet.

There was a Thog in the bright circle. It rolled rapidly out of the light and disappeared somewhere along the wall.

When the module's lights still hadn't come back on after several minutes, Jerry said, "We need to reach the power generator and see if we can manually restart it."

"That's over in Logistics and Utilities," DeShawn said.

Nan stepped ahead of Jerry, following her flashlight's beam through the transfer node. The computer-dog brushed against her legs, letting her know it was with them. Oort One had gravity because it rotated, but it was less than Earth's gravity. Fast walking made a person clumsy, and running was even worse. It was easy to lose control and go bounding around.

She stopped in the connecting corridor.

Right by the transfer node into the LUM, a girl of about thirteen crouched. She had short, jet black hair and she looked very scared. She was holding something close to her.

Something furry. A Thog.

"Yumiko! What're you doing with that creature?" Ailee's voice came out as a shriek. "You know better!"

Yumiko opened her hands and the creature bounced free. A second later, something slithered off her knees. Nan pointed the flashlight at the girl's feet. Another Thog slid over her legs to the ground and rolled away.

"It just had a baby," Yumiko said in a very small voice. "They—they're cute. I thought—they weren't doing any harm. So I picked one up, and suddenly—suddenly there were two in my hands."

Then the lights came blazing back on, and everybody shielded their eyes against the sudden glare. Nan turned the flashlight off.

"So far, whatever the Thogs mess up rights itself in time," DeShawn explained. "The station was designed to be self-repairing."

"But we're very afraid that something's going to happen that won't correct itself," Ailee added. "And if it happens to something important, like the life support systems—"

Ailee didn't explain what she feared might happen, but Nan could imagine. How long would it take to evacuate all the kids on the station if that happened? The trip from Edge Two had taken two hours. And the shuttle was too small to carry everybody at once, so that meant at least four hours before they could get everybody away. It was too scary to think about. They had to work on other plans.

"I'm sorry," Yumiko said, her eyes filling with tears. "I didn't know it was going to reproduce."

"How did it do that, exactly?" Nan wanted to know.

"I don't know," Yumiko said. "One minute I had one cuddled in my hand, then it sort of . . . shivered, I guess. And then it was kind of like it blew itself apart. Then there were two of them."

"You know never to touch them at all," Ailee scolded gently.

"I won't touch them again," Yumiko promised. "It's just that I miss my own pets at home."

"These aren't pets, Yumiko," DeShawn said. "But perhaps it's time to send you home? Someone else can take your place." He turned to Nan and Jerry. "We usually rotate the younger ones in the crew regularly because they get homesick. But this crisis has been so stressful they don't last long at all."

As the girl walked away, Ailee reminded them, "A lot of the younger kids think the Thogs are cute. It's hard to convince them there could be any danger in petting one."

"The sooner we get rid of them the better," Jerry said.

Nan agreed with that. She looked down at the computer-dog to see if it had any suggestions. It was standing like a statue, eyes glassy. "What happened to Arti?"

Ailee glanced down. "Oh. That's alien overload. He's thinking about the Thogs."

Ailee bent over to the AI and touched a spot on his neck right behind his ear.

"Interesting phenomenon," Arti said, blinking his eyes at them. "The Thogs are juveniles too, as one would expect. But they obviously reproduce at an earlier age than humans do. That's going to make them even more of a problem for us."

"Great!" Jerry said. "Even if we stop any more from hitchhiking aboard Oort One, their numbers are going to grow."

Nan turned her attention back to the Thogs. "Have you tried trapping them?"

DeShawn glanced at her. "What do you mean?"

"Putting out a cage with bait in it," she said.

"We don't like putting things in cages. It seems cruel," Ailee explained.

Will groaned. "The Thogs be vermin!"

"They're not very smart," DeShawn agreed. "Maybe they'd roll into a trap."

"What we need to do is—" Nan began.

"Here's what we're going to do," Jerry interrupted her. "I want everybody to scout around for things we can use to make a bunch of traps. All we need, really, is a basic box with a gate that we can rig to fall into place when a Thog walks in. I can figure out how to do that easily. And we'll try all sorts of food for bait till we find what works."

She was annoyed. The traps were her idea and here was Jerry taking over as if he'd thought of it. He seemed totally oblivious of what he'd done, but that didn't change things.

"Do we know what Thogs eat?" she asked.

Ailee and DeShawn looked at each other blankly.

"Now that you ask," DeShawn said, "the answer is no."

"Then we're going to have to find out," she said.

DeShawn was silent for a moment. Then he said, "There's lots of stuff stowed in the storage compartments on the lower deck of the LUM. That'd be a good place to start looking for trap-building material.

I'll show you where it is, but then I'd better get back to my job. Don't want to let any comets slip by while we're not paying attention.''

He seemed like a nice guy, and Nan was sorry she'd embarrassed him. To make up for it, she asked, ''What happens if they do?''

''A couple of big ones slammed into the Earth a few years ago, and they killed a lot of people,'' DeShawn said. ''Our job is to prevent it from happening again.''

''Will and I can make up some samples from the synthesizer robot in the galley,'' Ailee put in. ''Arti, come with us. I'll need you too.''

''Good,'' Jerry said. ''Nan, you and I will go with DeShawn and get the traps made.''

Will, Ailee, and Arti went back to the Habitat module. DeShawn headed through the transfer node into the LUM, and Jerry started to follow. Nan stood exactly where she was.

''What's the matter?'' Jerry asked when he realized she wasn't with him.

''I don't like being ordered about,'' she answered.

Jerry stared at her. He obviously didn't understand what was wrong. ''But I'm the team leader. It's my job to give the orders. It's not just because you're a girl.''

She frowned. ''You've forgotten something, Team Leader.''

''What's that?'' he asked.

''The bait in a rat trap is usually poisoned.'' She couldn't believe he hadn't thought of this.

''Are you two coming?'' DeShawn called.

''You can get back to your work, DeShawn,'' Jerry yelled. ''We'll find the storage compartments. There's something we have to settle here first.''

"If you don't use poisoned bait, how're you going to get rid of the Thogs afterwards?" she asked.

Jerry'd gone a little pale. He really was a wimp, she thought; like a lot of brainy kids he was afraid of fights.

"I admit I hadn't thought about that yet," he said. "But I would've thought of it in a while."

Jerry was skinny, and he hadn't done very well in Master Lobo's martial arts class. She could throw him easily if she wanted to teach him a lesson about team leadership. But Grampa Hong had taught her kung fu was not about hurting people.

"Look," Jerry began. "I didn't mean to steal your idea—"

"Yeah. I know," she said. "Way I see it, you're older than me and probably smarter, I'll give you that. But I'm stronger and quicker. I could drop you in a second. So I'd make a better team leader."

A small sound behind her made her turn. DeShawn was watching them with a horrified expression on his face. She realized the guy thought she was going to make good on her threat to drop Jerry right then. The idea came to her that maybe she should pretend to do it anyway just to see his face. She couldn't help grinning as she imagined his reaction. These future people were bigger wimps than Jerry!

She moved her hand up as if she were going to strike, and DeShawn's eyes glazed over.

"If we're going to defeat the Thogs, we've got to get one thing settled." At the last second she winked at Jerry, letting him in on the joke. "Neither of us orders the other one about."

Jerry smiled broadly and grabbed the hand she was holding out. "I accept that."

DeShawn sighed loudly with relief. "For a moment

there, Nan, I thought you were really going to hurt him.''

"Nah," she said, shrugging. "If I'd been serious, you wouldn't have seen my hand move."

"I know that's true!" Jerry said. "And now, Co-Leader, let's get to work fighting Thogs."

She hesitated for just a second. She'd never shared leadership with anybody before. Do it alone or don't do it at all had been her rule. But maybe she could give it a try.

"Right, Co-Leader," she replied. "We didn't come to the future just to have fun."

They both laughed at that.

DeShawn sighed. "I guess I'll never understand you two at all!"

15

"This has got to work," Jerry said.

He and Nan were sitting on the floor in the corridor in front of the storage compartments on the lower deck of the LUM. They had found a lot of useful material to make traps: plastic panels, sheets of aluminum, tubes of sealant for emergency repairs, and spools of wire.

"I'll draw up a plan for the traps, and then we're going to need a workbench to assemble them on," he said.

"The table in the galley ought to be big enough," Nan suggested. "Make the plan simple and even the younger kids can help build them."

They grabbed two large storage crates with wheels and stuffed all the material into them. Nan added measuring and cutting tools that she'd found in another of the compartments.

They wheeled the loaded crates to the circular staircase. The crates had to go on a small freight elevator beside the stairs. Then they went through the transfer node again and down the connecting corridor to the Habitat module where the galley was located.

In the galley, they found Ailee and Will and some of the station kids in the middle of a huge mess. Pots of weird looking stuff in different colors and textures sat around on the table and the floor. Some of it was still steaming, and an assortment of peculiar smells arose from the bowls. Jani, a thirteen-year-old they'd been introduced to yesterday, was stirring a pot of blood red goo she'd just got from the synthesizer.

One of the 'bots trundled around, carrying things, mostly getting in everybody's way. These 'bots weren't as intelligent as Arti, but all those arms and pincer-like hands could be useful. Arti was sitting to one side, watching everything intently, doing nothing. Jerry hoped he wasn't going into alien-overload again.

"Phew!" Nan said, wrinkling her nose. "This is supposed to attract Thogs?"

"We know not what Thogs eat, therefore we know not what attracts them," Will said reasonably. "Perchance they will like the smells, perchance the colors."

"I think we've got a real problem here, lack of info," Jerry said. "Don't you know anything about the Thogs except that they disrupt the electronics?"

Ailee sounded defensive. "We haven't had much time."

"Does the computer have any information on them?" he asked.

"No," Ailee said. "Nobody had ever seen Thogs before they showed up on this station, so nobody could put the information into the computer."

He shook his head without saying anything. It didn't sound like the ideal way to run a space station to him.

"Maybe the Thogs'll just be curious and want to know what the bait is," Jani added.

"We programmed the synthesizer to produce a variety of textures, tastes and aromas," Ailee explained.

"But of course we have no way of knowing the range of their sense of smell—or even if they have one. And we can't program something we don't know about."

He felt uneasy. There were too many things they didn't know about the Thogs.

"We kept a list of just what everything is so we can repeat the ones that work," Jani said.

"Good thinking, Jani." Jerry stuck a finger cautiously into a puddingy, lime-green mass, then put it to his lips. "Tastes a bit like key lime pie with a lot of oatmeal thrown in."

Nan said in a disgusted tone, "You're either brave or stupid, tasting something that looks like that!"

"There's no danger for humans," Arti explained. "The food synthesizer is actually a robot with limited abilities. And no 'bot can ever do anything that would harm humans. It's in their programming."

"I've read about that," Jerry said. "The Three Laws of Robotics, isn't it?"

"Well, we did start with that idea," Arti said. "But we found it had limits, so we modified it."

Jerry borrowed a palm-size computer from one of the kids and drew a diagram on the tiny screen of what he wanted the traps to look like.

"We need to assemble the sides like this, with the front side pulled up." He pointed to the screen. "Then we need to make a little mechanism like this one here that will be triggered by the Thog's entry to break, dropping the front down and trapping it inside the box."

"That e-pad's much too small to see." Ailee touched something on the e-pad, and the diagram appeared enlarged on one wall of the galley.

Everybody studied it, asking questions and making

suggestions. Jerry improved the plan until he was satisfied with it.

The galley immediately turned into a bustling workroom. The kids worked quickly and politely, with none of the pushing and shoving he'd have expected from a bunch of guys working in a crowded space in his own time. No one complained either.

The lights flickered once or twice as they worked, reminding them of the reason for the traps, but the pests who were menacing Oort One seemed to be taking it easy.

"Here, Yumiko," Ailee said, holding out a side of another trap she was making. "Take this for your trap while I check the bait."

The black-haired girl held a hand out and took the trap.

"What's the matter with your hand?" Ailee asked. She caught Yumiko's hand in hers and turned it over. "How did you get that rash? Did you touch a hot pot or something?"

Jerry leaned over to see the rash too. It didn't look too serious.

Yumiko shook her head. "I don't know. It doesn't hurt."

"You should get the medibot to look at it," Ailee advised.

"I will," the girl promised. "But I'm going home tomorrow."

The 'bot was very useful cutting tough material and spot welding, and the traps began to take shape. As each one was finished, Nan tested it by cautiously pushing something inside and checking that the front gate came down immediately. If a Thog entered, it would be trapped.

"Wait a minute. What if they can open the traps?"

Nan asked. "A raccoon probably could. Maybe even a clever gerbil."

"They don't have hands like a raccoon," Ailee replied. "So if they roll inside and the gate comes down, they won't be able to get back out."

"We need to do this scientifically," Jerry said. "The traps need to be numbered, and we'll have to keep track of which bait went into which trap."

"The 'bot can engrave numbers on the traps," Ailee said.

When that was done, Will and Jani put glops of the bait into them while Ailee made a list on the e-pad of what went into each one. Finally there was a long line of traps ready to be distributed all over the station to catch Thogs. Everybody in the galley helped load the two rolling storage carts.

One boy with long blond hair hesitated in the doorway with his cart and asked, "What's going to happen to the Thogs when we find them in the traps?"

"Good question, Riki," Ailee said. She turned to look at Jerry for the answer.

The thing they didn't want to do was let the captured Thogs get together to combine forces and harm the station. He'd been thinking of how to dispose of them one by one while everybody was busy making the traps.

Space was a vacuum, so if he ejected them through the airlock where the shuttle docked, they'd have no oxygen or anything else to breathe and that should take care of them. If they breathed. But then everything living had to breathe one way or another, didn't it? It was worth trying.

He explained this plan to the others.

"We'll have to eject them one at a time," Ailee said, sounding doubtful. "We wouldn't dare put more

90

than one in the lock at the same time or they'd roll into a ball and wreck it. It'll be a long process.''

"Kill the enemies as we catch them!" Will agreed cheerfully. "Like tossing Spaniards overboard!"

Jerry had noticed Will's bloodthirsty mind. He'd thought Drake and his men were wonderful, heroic figures, sailing around the world in their little ship. Maybe they were heroes, but they were pirates too.

"Will, I really think you should reconsider these hostile remarks," Ailee said seriously. "Everybody is entitled to respect, no matter where they come from. And there are some kids on this station who have ancestors from Spain. It's not nice to hurt their feelings by constantly talking about killing Spaniards."

"The truth of the matter," Arti put in, "is that Sir Francis Drake didn't toss too many people overboard at all."

Will glared at the computer-dog. Jerry hid his smile.

"You mean, you're really going to *kill* the Thogs?" Riki asked in a shaky voice.

"Well, yes," Jerry said. "They're pests, aren't they?"

"Enemies," Will said stubbornly.

Riki looked glum at that. Ailee patted him on the shoulder and the team headed out to place the traps.

"I can see why they needed us," Nan murmured, passing Jerry. "They're too soft-hearted to help themselves!"

16

Next morning, Nan had some real doubts that Jerry's idea of tossing Thogs through the airlock would work. In the first place, it was a big "if" that the baited traps they'd set out last night would even work. Nobody knew what Thogs ate to stay alive. And even if the traps did work, Ailee was right: It was going to be a slow process.

She thought about it as she dressed in the cabin she shared with Ailee who'd already gone off to check the traps.

First you put a Thog in the airlock. Then you lock the inner doors. Then you open the outer doors and the Thog gets sucked out into space. Next you relock the outer doors, equalize the air pressure, open the inner doors, and dump in another Thog. Then you repeat the whole process.

Coming through the lock after the shuttle trip from Edge Two had taken several minutes before they could go through onto the space station. How long was it going to take to get rid of even a few Thogs? But they didn't dare put more than one in at a time or the things might unite to jam the mechanism of the airlock.

There had to be a better way.

She saw something move out of the corner of her eye. She turned away from the mirror where she'd been braiding her dark hair. There. She saw it again in the corner of the cabin, under Ailee's desk. It moved again.

Her breath caught in her throat. Holding the edge of the bunk to steady herself, she bent down to see what it was.

A Thog. Here, in her cabin. Her heart pounded in her chest.

Don't be stupid! she told herself. Thogs didn't attack. And as long as there was only one Thog under there it couldn't do any harm. Yumiko had been cuddling one of them and its baby, and nothing had happened to her.

Curiosity took over from her first feelings of fright. She knelt down by the desk. Slowly, she extended her hand a little way toward the Thog. It didn't move. She peered at it. It actually looked cute. Cuddly, like a round, fat, Persian kitten. A kitten with no feet and no face. Her hand moved a bit further.

Contact.

She jerked her hand back. It was like getting a tiny electric shock, the kind you get from dragging your feet across a thick carpet then touching a metal door handle. She tried again. This time her fingers felt fur, warm and soft. The little thing meant no harm. Maybe humans just misunderstood Thogs.

Pick me up. Hold me.

Those weren't her thoughts! They were coming from the Thog. She tore her hand away, and the thoughts stopped.

When Ailee said, "They pull this mental effect," Nan had been very scornful. Now she understood what Ailee meant. No wonder the kids on the station had trouble taking the threat seriously. The aliens affected the way they thought. But these little things weren't harmless; in large numbers they might be dangerous enough to kill humans.

There had to be a way to get rid of Thogs if the airlock idea didn't work. And of course there was a way. Poison. They had to eat something, right? That seemed obvious even though she had no idea where their mouths were. If the Thogs were dead when they were taken out of the traps, then you could put as many as you liked into the airlock at one time.

A long time ago, she remembered, their apartment in Santa Marta had a bad problem with mice. Ti kept parakeets, and their birdseed got spilled all over the floor as they ate, attracting the rodents. What had her stepfather used as bait to get rid of them? It was a kind of cheesy paste that he spread on bread crusts, and then had to wash his hands carefully to get the toxic residue off. But what was in the paste?

Doctor Chen had taught them how to access Library, the unit of the central computer that kept all the information anybody could ever want. There was a terminal in the cabin; she sat down at Ailee's desk to use it.

The cabin lights went out. The emergency lighting sputtered, then it went out too. Nan pulled the flashlight out of her pocket again. The beam picked out a lone Thog slowly crossing the floor. As soon as the light touched it, the Thog picked up speed and disappeared into a dark corner.

This time both sets of lights stayed out for several seconds before they flickered and came on again. She hastily shut off the flashlight, conserving the battery. Who knew how many times she'd have to use it before they solved the problem for good? She set it carefully on the desk. How long did it take a Thog to grow up enough to reproduce? They didn't have to be adults, Arti said.

She entered the code Doctor Chen had taught them to use.

"Ready," said a warm female voice in the empty cabin.

"Library," she said. It still amazed her that the computers here sounded like real people, not like the robot voice she heard in her own time when she phoned Directory Assistance, reading out the telephone number she'd asked for.

"One moment. Accessing Library now."

Then the voice changed to a deeper male one. "Library. Hello, Nan. What do you wish to know?"

"I need to know what was in a rodent poison my stepfather used to get rid of mice. He made a paste. I don't know what the ingredients were."

"One moment."

She pulled out an e-pad to record the "recipe." The overhead light flickered. She stared up at it, but nothing else happened.

Then Library said, "Rodenticides in use at the end of the twentieth century, and typically administered in paste form, include phosphorus, barium carbonate salt, zinc phosphide, white arsenic—"

"Wait! Slow down! I can't type that quickly."

"No need to write them down, Nan," Library said kindly. "I'll transfer the list to the e-pad for you."

She glanced at the e-pad in her hand. Tiny letters now scrolled up the miniature screen . . . *Arsenic, thallium sulfate, strychnine . . .*

"Can I be of any further help, Nan?" Library asked.

"Not at the moment."

She slipped the e-pad in her pocket and ran to the galley. All the time they'd been training at the center in Kern, it had felt like a game, a lark, some kind of grand adventure she'd fallen into. Suddenly it was real and as grim as a bad dream. People could get killed on this adventure. Maybe even somebody on her team.

The galley was empty when she reached it. She'd expected some of the station kids might be there hanging around after breakfast. That's what she and Ti liked to do on the weekends when they didn't have to rush off to school. Those days with Ti seemed very far away.

For a moment she felt alone and very homesick. Not for Oak House, and not even for the apartment where her mother and the new boyfriend were probably drugged out right now. But she missed her brother.

"In the end there will be good fortune," Grampa's voice seemed to say in her memory. All she had to do was the very best she could.

She took out the e-pad. The words were so tiny on the miniature screen she had to squint to read them at all. She was afraid she'd make a mistake and order the synthesizer to make the wrong thing. Her hands were shaking with nerves.

Something about the word "strychnine" seemed familiar. Was that what her stepfather had used? She decided to try that one first. She turned her attention to the synthesizer. One button was marked ON. That seemed simple enough. She depressed it and a red light came on.

What amount to make? An ounce? A pound? An ounce sounded safe. Now she began slowly entering the word for the poison onto the synthesizer's control pad, being careful to get the spelling right. The entry showed up in a small window above the panel. Under the ON button was another one that said ENTER. One last check that the word was spelled correctly, then she pressed it carefully with her index finger. Another red light lit.

Then all the lights went out in the galley, including those on the synthesizer.

17

"There's a way to manually jiggle the power generator that sometimes gets it going again," DeShawn said. "It's supposed to fix itself, but whatever the Thogs are doing, it's taking longer and longer to self-repair."

He and Jerry were on their hands and knees on the floor of the cramped service space below the deck on the Logistics and Utilities module. The dim lighting from the emergency system was even dimmer here. Whoever designed Oort One hadn't expected people to need to come down here very often, Jerry figured. Not only was the crawl space narrow, but there were support struts and wall braces all over the place. A fully grown man couldn't possibly maneuver his way through.

"Ah," DeShawn said. "See that box? Inside we should find what we're looking for."

Doctor Pike had mentioned this manual restart switch in the training sessions on the model of the space station. Oort One was so far away from the sun that solar power wouldn't work; the generator De-Shawn was tinkering with operated by nuclear fusion. The thought made Jerry's skin crawl. This is the future, he reminded himself; they've got the bugs ironed out of nuclear power now. He certainly hoped they had.

"Hold this flap up for me, Jerry, while I reach in here. Got it!" DeShawn said as the lights came back on.

"Ouch!" Jerry hit his head on a metal strut as he tried to turn around in the narrow space. "Let's get out of here and go check traps."

Arti was waiting for them at the entrance.

"Well done," Arti said.

"De nada!" DeShawn said, grinning. "I'd love to check traps, Jerry, but I ought to monitor the telescope. Sometimes these power blips mess up the programming. Wouldn't want a monster comet to slip past while we weren't paying attention."

DeShawn took off for the science module, while Jerry and the computer dog crossed the narrow corridor that connected the LUM to the command module.

Arti glanced up at Jerry. "You seem to be in good spirits."

He smiled. "I was rehearsing my speech to Doctor Pike about how they can prepare teams better if they have to do something like this again."

As they entered the command module, he had a new thought. "They were amazingly organized when they yanked us. The whole training system was in place like they'd done this before. We're not the first team, are we?"

"Correct," Arti said. "The Thogs are a new menace, but we've had problems with aliens prior to this."

"What happened to those kids?" he asked.

"They went back to their own times, just as you will when this is all over."

"I would've thought stories like theirs would make front page in the *National Enquirer!*" he said. "But I'm forgetting. You couldn't let them go back talking about the future."

"We gave them an amnesia drug," Arti admitted.

"So there are a bunch of kids in my time who don't know they've been here to the future? How many?"

Before Arti could answer, Ailee marched around a thin partition that separated the work cubicles. She pushed two younger kids, a boy and a girl, ahead of her, and she carried an armload of Thog traps. He recognized one of the kids, Riki.

"Just look at this!" Ailee showed Jerry the empty traps.

"There's no bait in them," he said, not sure what was going on.

"No. But there was last night." Ailee gestured at the two kids who were staring at the floor and shuffling their feet in embarrassment. "And this morning there were Thogs in the traps."

"The bait worked?" Jerry asked. "But that's great! Which samples—" He broke off, aware of Ailee's displeasure.

"How could you?" Ailee turned to the two kids. "You know how dangerous the Thogs are. You know what happened to—to—" She stopped and looked at Jerry.

"It's okay," he said. "I heard about the accident."

"These two found Thogs in the traps this morning," Ailee went on. "And they let them go."

"But Ailee," the girl said. "You were going to kill them."

"They aren't a problem one by one," Riki argued. "Couldn't we just try to keep them apart?"

Ailee groaned and ran both hands through her red curls.

Jerry could see this was going to be a real difficulty. It was hard to get the crew on Oort One to accept the fact that the Thogs had to be destroyed. It was okay while they were making traps and brewing bait and just talking about it, but as soon as they had to physically put a Thog in the airlock and kill it, they'd balk. He had a sinking feeling that Ailee, smart as she was, might be just as reluctant as these two given the chance.

As he stood wondering what to do next, Will appeared with a smile as bright as a lighthouse, his arms loaded with traps. Each one contained a Thog. Will showed off his catch.

"Be this not a marvel?" Will said jauntily. "And it mattered not what bait we used. They loved it all."

He dumped the traps at Jerry's feet and the kids began protesting.

"Don't drop them like that!"

"You'll hurt the poor little things!"

Will stopped smiling. "These be your enemies."

"Enemies feel pain too," the girl said, sniffing back tears.

Grim-faced, Will picked up traps.

Jerry glanced down at Arti.

"Luckily," Arti said, "the airlock is free for use."

Jerry scooped up the rest of the traps and everybody went through the transfer node to the end of the corridor where Airlock A was located. He stood by the control panel, ignoring the wailing behind him. He could hear Ailee hushing the kids up, but it didn't sound to him that her heart was in it. Any minute now he was afraid she'd burst into tears too. Great! They were only at the beginning of this mission and he was losing control of his team already.

The inner door of the airlock cycled open and Will emptied the first of the six captive Thogs out of the trap and into the lock. A light on the panel turned red. Then he twisted the knob on the outer door control and a second red light lit.

The wailing behind Jerry had stopped. He turned and saw Ailee standing alone in the corridor.

"I sent Riki and Kelda away," she said. "No point in them watching."

Jerry waited for the airlock to go through its cycle. Finally, the control panel showed a green light. He opened the airlock's door, Will dumped another Thog inside, and he repeated the process. This wasn't turning out the way Jerry'd envisioned it. He should've guessed that if the solution was going to be this easy the Oort One crew would've found it for themselves and wouldn't have needed kids from the past.

It was a long, slow process getting rid of six Thogs. When he and Will had finished, Jerry turned and found Ailee still there. Her face was pale and her expression stony, but she hadn't run away from the nasty work they'd had to do.

"Thanks for standing by us, Ailee," he said.

"Methinks we need a different solution," Will said. "This be tiresome work."

"I think you're right," Jerry agreed. He felt shaken up inside. As soon as he had a chance, he wanted to talk this through with Arti.

Just then, a 'bot rolled to a stop beside Will and one of its metal extensions reached out to the boy, giving him something about the size of a baseball.

"If I be not needed here," Will said to Jerry, "then

I would go with the talking box to seek refreshment in pleasant pastimes."

"You can think of recreation at a time like this?" Ailee asked.

"Let him go," Jerry said. "We need a new plan. And I've got a lot of thinking to do before I come up with one."

18

More than a minute passed this time before the lights came back on. A minute was a long time, Nan thought, when you were all alone in the darkness on a space station a very long way from home. By the time light finally flooded the galley again, her heart was racing uncomfortably.

Something rolled around the corner from the corridor and into the galley. She jumped. It was about the right size for a large Thog. But it wasn't a Thog; it was a ball and it seemed to be made of wood. Frowning, she squatted down to take a look at it—and was almost knocked over backward by the 'bot that came trundling after it.

"Hey! Watch where you're going!" she said.

The robot's eye stalk swiveled to look at her; then one of its pincerlike hands extended and grabbed up the ball.

"Sorry," its voicebox squawked.

"What're you doing here anyway?" she asked.

Now Will ran around the corner and tumbled in a clumsy halt beside the 'bot.

"I warned you about the effects of the station's low gravity," she said.

Will laughed and picked himself up. "The talking

box and I play at bowls. And I claim the victory!''

He was carrying another ball the same size as the one the 'bot had pursued.

"Where did you get those wooden balls?" she asked.

"The talking box did make them," Will said. "But by my troth, they be not well balanced! Nor be they true wood. Come, Nan, I will show you the game."

She shook her head. "Not right now. I've got something I ought to be doing—"

"Nay. What be the words you say? Take a break!" Will urged.

She laughed. Will and the 'bot went out of the galley; she stood in the doorway watching.

"Now," Will said, taking a much smaller ball from a pocket of his jumpsuit. "I shall place the jack on the course in the position where it last stood."

He trotted away from her and gently set the smaller ball down close to the transfer node at the end of the corridor. Then he came back.

"And now, I take the chance, by virtue of winning the first game," Will said. "Thus!"

He bent one knee and bowled the larger ball toward the jack. It stopped about three inches away. Then the 'bot took its turn bowling its ball—which went straight into one wall, ricocheted off, passed the jack, hit the other wall and came rolling back almost to Nan's feet.

"I don't know what the object of this game is," she said, giggling. "But I don't think much of your competition, Will."

"The talking box learns fast," Will said seriously. "Yet I have the best ball. And he shall play again."

Puzzled, she asked, "Aren't both balls the same?"

Will looked equally confused. "Verily, they be the

same weight and heft. But my wood hath come closer to the jack, wherefore I said I have the best ball. So he doth play first.''

She shook her head. "Crazy game! Did you invent it?''

Will looked shocked. "Nay! My captain and the other captains—verily, even the admiral!—do often-times play at bowls on Plymouth Hoe.''

"Well," she said, "I'll leave you two to your game. I have work to do.''

She went back into the galley and gazed at the synthesizer. The power failure had voided the instructions she'd been entering and she had to begin all over again.

Strychnine.

She misspelled the word several times. Finally she got it right and pressed the ENTER button.

Nothing happened for several seconds. Then the red light above the button began blinking and the window which had displayed the word she'd just entered now contained a message:

UNABLE TO SYNTHESIZE.

She frowned at it. "Why not?''

Ailee said the synthesizer could make anything, and she'd demonstrated, producing pizzas and chocolate cake, grilled cheese sandwiches, milk, fruit, whatever anybody asked for. By some process Nan didn't understand, the synthesizer 'bot seemed to make something out of nothing. No wonder Will, who knew less about science than Nan herself, called it magic! But maybe there was some ingredient in strychnine that the machine didn't have. What was in it, anyhow? She'd never been good in chemistry class. She glanced at the other words that Library had dug out for her. Here was one with salt in it. That was common enough. Try that.

She entered, "Barium carbonate salt."

She pressed ENTER. Seconds passed. The red light blinked.

UNABLE TO SYNTHESIZE.

"What's the matter with the dumb thing?" she grumbled.

Will came into the galley, clutching his bowling ball, and stood beside her. He watched silently as she typed in another choice: arsenic.

"What happened to the bowling match?" she asked

Will shrugged his shoulders. "There be little amusement in winning every game."

She smiled. "You're right about that!"

Arsenic seemed a simple enough request. Surely the synthesizer could provide that? Now that she thought of it, arsenic went into the insecticides that Mrs. Turner used in the kitchen of Oak House to kill roaches. She typed it in, remembering the lectures about how the girls needed to be careful not to get it on their hands because it was so poisonous.

UNABLE TO SYNTHESIZE.

"What do you with the food thing, Nan?" Will asked.

"Trying to make a poison to kill Thogs. But the synthesizer 'bot isn't cooperating."

"There be many wonders in this beauteous new world," Will commented. "Yet methinks these things called 'bots be not perfect."

She stared at the synthesizer. Maybe it had been damaged by the last power failure. She considered for a second, then typed more words into its pad and pressed the button.

This time a green light came on, the door popped open, and a steaming hot plate of blueberry pancakes waited for her. So that answered the question about damage. She took the plate out carefully. Might as well eat the pancakes; she'd missed breakfast.

"A slice of prime ham to that, prithee, and I shall join you," Will said.

She typed his order in. When it was ready, they both sat at the table where only a few hours ago they'd been stuffing bait into the traps. The pancakes were light and fluffy, just as she liked them. Maple syrup. Butter. They tasted delicious. Will ate his ham with obvious pleasure.

While she ate, she mulled over something that had begun to bother her. She'd had enemies before. Tank and her partner at Oak House came to mind, but there'd been others. And they always wanted something from you; they were either on a power trip and wanted to boss you around, or they wanted your stuff. Or both.

What did the Thogs want from humans? Why were they invading the space station? If they had the power to mess it up the way they did, they could probably build themselves all the space stations they needed. Why invade this one? She couldn't see the answer to that, but she had a feeling it could be important. If they could figure it out, maybe they'd have a better handle on defeating the aliens.

When she'd cleared her plate, she stared at the synthesizer again.

"I'll give you one more try," she told the 'bot, although she knew it couldn't hear or understand anything that wasn't typed into its control pad.

She stood up and typed in *Phosphorus paste.*"

She wasn't surprised to read, UNABLE TO SYNTHE-SIZE.

"I wasn't planning on eating the stuff, you know!" she said, irritated at its stupidity.

"Why doth the thing not do its magic to serve you?" Will asked.

"Because it's dumb!" she replied.

It was no use. Arti had told them the secret of the synthesizer 'bot: It was unable to do anything that might harm humans. Now she realized it was too lim-ited in its abilities to be able to figure out that she needed the poison for Thogs, not herself. These ma-chines were wonderful, but they weren't smart like Arti. She guessed it wasn't practical to build advanced artificial intelligence into every little machine on the space station.

Back to square one, she thought. Get a new plan, Nan.

"Perchance now you will play at bowls with me?" Will asked hopefully. "I shall teach you to play better than the talking box!"

Just then, her e-pad gave a small *ting!* She looked down and read the message scrolling over its small screen.

"No time for bowls. Jerry wants us," she told Will. "He's called a strategy meeting in the command mod-ule."

Leaving the galley, they caught sight of a Thog sitting in the corridor about where Will's jack had been a few minutes earlier. Immediately, Will stooped and launched his wooden ball at it. But the alien slid out of the way at the last second and the ball passed harmlessly.

"Close, but no cigar," she said.

Will gave her a puzzled glance.

"Never mind," she said. "Figure that it means we need a better solution, so we'd better start thinking. This is one game we have to win."

19

When Will and Nan came into the command module, Jerry could tell from Nan's expression there was something major wrong. Hah, he thought. Put it on the list. There was a lot of bad news ahead of it. He glanced at DeShawn, leaning against a desk, looking grim. He'd called DeShawn away from his telescope for this meeting.

Will sat down crosslegged on the floor, and picked up a length of thin aluminum piping that lay where a passing 'bot had dropped it. He flexed it experimentally, his expression thoughtful. Ailee watched him, running her hands through her curly hair, something Jerry'd observed her doing a lot when she was worried. Arti lay down beside them and put his nose on his paws. Nan slumped into a swivel chair near Will and folded her arms across her chest. Everybody waited for Jerry to begin.

"We've got some problems to discuss," he said. "There's something going on we don't understand."

Nan looked as if she were about to say something, so he waited. But she didn't, so he quickly brought her up to speed, running through the scene with the trapped Thogs, the unacceptable slowness of the airlock solution, and the station kids' reluctance to kill

111

Thogs. He was going to have to eat humble pie here, but leaders had to be able to put rivalries aside for the sake of their mission.

"So," he finished. "We're going to need to try something you suggested, Nan. Poisoned bait."

To his surprise, she didn't start gloating about being right. Instead she looked as if she'd picked the wrong box in some kind of guessing game.

"Can't be done," Nan said flatly. "Unless there's a supply of insecticide already on the station for roaches or ants."

"We don't have insects on the station," DeShawn explained. He seated himself on the edge of the desk and leaned forward. "Everything was sterilized before it was brought up here, and if something got through, then the vacuum conditions of the assembly period would've killed it. No insects, no insecticides."

"What about the synthesizer?" Jerry asked. But he knew what the answer was going to be the moment he asked the question.

Nan made a scowling face. "The synthesizer 'bot is programmed not to make anything that might harm humans. And it's so stupid it can't figure out we want to use poison on the Thogs, not on ourselves."

"There's always the chance of accidents," Arti murmured from his place on the floor. "Humans are sometimes shockingly careless. We needed to be careful."

"So you put a nursemaid in place to baby your people," Nan said scornfully. "People can't make their own decisions here, is that it? No wonder you need help from our time!"

Jerry thought about the fact that they were all kids on the space station. He could imagine what the adults back on Earth must be feeling like. They must be scared half to death having to send their kids out here into danger. Maybe that explained why now and again they ran into a grumpy one like Doctor Pike.

"Well, traps aren't going to work," he said, glancing round at the team. "Let's consider other options."

DeShawn and Ailee gazed back at him. He hoped they'd think he was being democratic, giving them all a chance to contribute. In reality, he didn't have a plan himself.

Before anyone could answer Jerry, Will held something up. "Here, my masters, be the bane of monstrous beasts."

Ailee frowned. "What is it?"

"A sling to kill Thogs," Will said.

Jerry looked at the slingshot Will had assembled out of a forked piece of aluminum strung with a length of rubber tubing. "Not bad. What will you use for shot?"

Will stood up. He rummaged in a pocket, then pulled out a wooden ball about the size of a golfball. "The jack shall serve."

He fitted it into the sling, then looked around for a target. A very small Thog chose that moment to roll across the floor at the end of the module. Will fired the ball. The Thog careened into a corner from the force of the shot and lay still.

"Yay, Will!" Nan said. "Looks like you've been hunting Thogs all your life."

"Nay," Will said modestly. "Squirrels, crows, and rabbits."

"That was fine, Will," Jerry said. "It really was. But unless you can make enough slingshots for all of us, and teach us to be as good marksmen as you, then it's going to take a long time to make much difference."

They were all silent for a moment after that, but Will loaded the ball into the sling again and peered around through narrowed eyes to spot another target.

Then Nan said, "We ought to try and figure out what the Thogs want. Enemies always want something from you."

"How can they want something unless they're intelligent?" Ailee asked. "Do you think they are?"

"I've no idea right now," Nan said. "But if we know what it is they want, maybe we can do something about it."

Will stopped surveying for Thogs. "Nan hath the right of it. Thy enemy seeks either to kill thee, or take thy ship or thy treasure, or all three."

"We don't have any treasure," Ailee said doubtfully.

"Yes, we do," DeShawn said. "Earth itself is our treasure. Maybe it's not Oort One they want, except as a gateway to Earth."

"Then why didn't they jump straight through the t-ports?" Ailee asked. "Why did they stop here first?"

"That might've been a mistake," Jerry suggested. "Perhaps they didn't realize you were coming here when they hitchhiked with you."

"They're not very bright," DeShawn agreed.

"They're juveniles," Arti said. He closed his eyes.

Nan swung her swivel chair back and forth for a moment. Then she said, "There has to be a way to defeat them. I don't see it just yet, but we'd all better do some serious thinking."

Before anyone could say anything else, the lights dimmed again. They sat for a minute waiting. Finally the emergency lights glowed a dim yellow.

"We can't let this go on," Jerry said.

"We had rats on the *Hind*," Will said. "They swarmed up the mooring lines, carrying filth and sickness with them."

"What did you do about them?" Ailee asked.

"Cats." Will stuffed his slingshot into a back pocket. "A mariner carried a brace of cats aboard. In sooth, the cats hunted the rats and that was the end of it."

"I thought people in your time believed only witches kept cats?" Jerry said.

"Captain Drake be too wise for such nonsense," Will explained. "And he learned a trick or two from the Moors we encountered on Africa's western coast. We have one such on board, darker of face than Master DeShawn, he be."

Jerry glanced at Nan.

"It's worth a try," Nan said.

"Arti?" he asked.

The computer-dog opened one steel-gray eye. "Personally, I despise felines. Silly creatures, if you want my opinion. But go ahead."

"Ailee," Jerry said, "If we send somebody back through the t-ports to Kern, do you think we could get maybe a couple of dozen cats in a hurry? Would people lend us their pets?"

"Would they be in any danger?" Ailee asked. "People wouldn't want their pets to go into danger."

"What be the life of a cat compared to that of a man?" Will sounded incredulous. "Verily—"

Nan put a hand on Will's arm, hushing him.

"Cats are much bigger than Thogs," Jerry pointed out. "I don't see a problem."

"But I do," DeShawn said. "What if adult cats are like adult humans in the t-ports?"

Ailee's face went white. "That would be terrible!"

"And kittens may be safe to t-port, but they wouldn't be much use hunting Thogs," Nan added.

Yet it was too good an idea to give up so easily, Jerry thought. "All right. Get half-grown cats. Cats that aren't too big to travel through the t-ports, but are big enough to hunt."

"I'll radio our request to Kern immediately," DeShawn said. "The 'bots can bring cats through the t-ports."

"Little cats might be frightened by 'bots," Ailee said. She stood up. "I'll go fetch them myself."

"You sure that's necessary?" Nan asked.

Ailee nodded. "I wouldn't want them to be scared. People will be more willing to let their cats go if they know I'm taking good care of them."

"DeShawn?" Jerry asked.

DeShawn shrugged his shoulders.

"And just in time, the shuttle has returned from Edge Two," Arti announced.

As he said this, three of the canister 'bots trundled through the transfer node out of the command module and headed for the airlock to unload the cargo the shuttle was carrying. The team followed.

Ailee stood with DeShawn by the airlock, waiting for the 'bots to finish their work. As Ailee stepped into the airlock, Nan said, "I sure hope this idea's going to work."

Jerry wasn't sure it would, but he didn't have a better idea to offer in its place.

"We'll just have to wait and see," he said.

20

As the airlock door closed behind Ailee, Nan looked at the other members of the team, who were still standing around looking dejected.

"Well, we might as well see if there are any more traps to empty," Jerry said finally. "No sense waiting here. It could be hours before Ailee gets back."

DeShawn said, "It's not the t-porting that takes time, just the shuttle trip to and from the t-port on Edge Two."

"And how long shall it take in the city to find goodwives who must lend us their cats?" Will asked.

Nobody answered him. Nan remembered the cat at Oak House; Tiger had come from the local pound. Did they have pounds and animal control officers in this future? Even if nobody abandoned their pets anymore or let them have unwanted litters, dogs and cats sometimes ran away or got lost. That couldn't have changed. Yet even in her century there were microchips to permanently identify pets and return them when they got lost, so there probably wouldn't be too many strays. It might take Ailee a long time to gather enough kittens of exactly the right age.

Just as the group turned to reenter the module to round up traps, a girl with short brown hair came hurrying through the transfer node from Habitat.

"Ailee! Ailee!" the girl called. "Where's Ailee?"

"She went on an errand," Jerry said.

"What is it, Jasmin?" DeShawn asked. "What's wrong?"

"The synthesizer won't work. It won't make food for us. And everybody's hungry," Jasmin announced.

Nan looked at Jerry. If there'd been another power failure caused by the Thogs recently, she hadn't noticed it. And if it had been such a small one that nobody noticed, then the synthesizer 'bot should have self-repaired quickly.

"We'll come and look at it," Jerry said.

Nan, Jerry, Will, and Arti went back to the galley in the habitat module with Jasmin, where they found a small crowd gathered around the food synthesizer. The galley was noisy with a babble of voices discussing what to do.

"Okay," Nan said, taking control. "Let's not have everybody talking at once. What's the problem?"

Riki spoke up. "It's not working at all. It won't even give us a red light to show it can't make something."

"It's never stopped working this long before," Kelda said.

"Perchance you commanded it to make vile green things?" Will asked.

Nan had noticed how suspicious Will was of eating salad. He'd told her that the men of his time didn't eat leaves. No amount of explaining had made him believe that stuff like lettuce and broccoli were edible, let alone healthy. He ate meat, bread, cheese and an occasional piece of fruit, which was what he was used to on the *Golden Hind*.

Jerry frowned at the control pad.

"Here," she said. "Let me do it."

Jerry stepped aside, and she typed in the same meal the synthesizer had made for her that morning, pancakes with maple syrup. Nothing happened. She tried bacon and scrambled eggs. Nothing. Pizza. Nothing. Jello. Nothing.

"Told you so," Riki said. "What're we going to do now?"

Kelda wailed. "The synthesizer robot is the only way we can make food on the station. Why would the Thogs do this to us? We never wanted to hurt them!"

"I want to go home," Jasmin said. She looked as if she were going to cry.

Another boy suddenly remembered he'd made a box of chocolate chip cookies one evening so he could have a late snack in his cabin. Now he generously offered to get them and share them.

"Good idea," Nan said. "Why don't you all go with Rod and eat cookies while we see what we can do?"

The kids ran off quickly, and Jerry glanced at Nan.

"You have a plan?" he asked.

She shrugged her shoulders. "No. But I'd rather discuss things with you two without an audience that gets hysterical so quickly. And Arti, of course," she added. She didn't know if an AI had feelings, but she didn't want to hurt them if it did.

"Think you this be the Thogs' doing?" Will asked.

Nan and Jerry both nodded.

"If this thing's anything like my mom's microwave oven," Jerry said, gazing at the synthesizer, "then it should have the cooking unit at the top or the back. Will, help me get it off the wall. I'll take a look at it."

When they finally managed to pry the synthesizer

away from the wall, two Thogs fell out and rolled away.

Will let go of the end of the synthesizer he was holding and grabbed for his slingshot.

"Hey!" Jerry yelled, staggering under the full weight.

"Do be careful!" Arti advised.

The Thogs disappeared. Will stuffed his slingshot away again and took up his share of the synthesizer. Together he and Jerry set it down on the floor.

But they found nothing at the back of the synthesizer except a long thin tube that disappeared into the wall. The tube wasn't thick enough for food to come through, Nan could see that. You couldn't possibly squeeze a pizza through. Not even Jello could make it. But the rest of the synthesizer was just a box, and she couldn't see how or where it prepared food.

"Magic makes the box to work!" Will insisted.

For once Nan was almost inclined to agree with him.

"No, it's future science," Jerry said. "I can't explain it, but I know it's not magic."

"Indeed not," Arti said. "The robots service the synthesizer regularly with a nutritious compound made up of the ingredients of just about anything anyone could wish to eat. Then the machine selects and mixes and serves up the food."

"Way cool!" Nan said. "We could use one of those at home."

"Do you suppose that compound is what the Thogs have been eating?" Jerry asked. "Have they been stealing our food?"

"Possibly," Arti said. "I'd need more data to be certain."

"Let's put it back and try again," Jerry suggested.

They got the synthesizer up on the wall, but it still wasn't working.

"The station isn't supposed to have breakdowns like this!" Jerry said.

"Famous last words," Nan commented. "Guaranteed not to break down."

"This could be a real nuisance," Jerry said. "It means we'll have to ask Edge Two if they have a spare synthesizer. If not, we'll have to send 'bots in the shuttle to bring back raw food supplies. That's going to be time consuming."

"We don't have another choice," she said. "But I suggest we send the younger kids back to Earth as well. For one thing, it'll be easier not to have to find food for so many. And for another, kids like Jasmin need to go home in any case."

"Good plan," Will agreed. "A small crew survives longer when victuals be scarce aboard ship."

"Okay," Jerry said. "Nan, can you make up a list of food supplies we'll need if Edge Two can't spare a synthesizer?"

"Can do," she said.

"Meanwhile, I shall hunt Thogs," Will suggested.

He was bouncing on his toes, full of energy. He clearly didn't like to stand still. Hunting Thogs sounded like the best thing for him to do until Ailee got back.

"You do that," Nan told him.

The guys and Arti left the galley on their errands and she sat down with her e-pad to start making up a food list. The fingertips of her right hand tingled as she touched the pad. She looked at them and frowned. A tiny patch of red spots had appeared on her three middle fingers. Where could they have come from? Her left hand was completely clear. They didn't hurt, just tingled when she made contact with something. No sense worrying about them.

For the first time since she'd left Oak House she realized she was glad for something she'd learned there. Mrs. Turner believed that all the girls should learn about running a home, and that had included making up a weekly grocery list for the eight girls who lived there and the staff counselors. She was willing to bet the House Mother would never have dreamed of feeding a space station's crew, but she'd taught Nan well how to estimate how much food each person required.

Her stomach rumbled. Better get used to being hungry, she thought. There was no way Ailee could get back to them in less than a day if she had to round up two dozen cats to bring with her. She began to type in her list.

21

Jerry hoped Ailee could find enough cats that were good hunters, or they'd have to face the choice of either starving or giving up the station and admitting they couldn't deal with the problem they'd been yanked into the future to solve.

The traps weren't working at all now. He guessed the aliens weren't intrigued by the bright colors and smells of the bait any more. He saw Thogs all over the modules, sliding under bunks and tables when people entered, sitting on shelves in storage areas, ducking out of sight into the air vents. They seemed to be reproducing faster than rabbits. Everywhere he looked, small furry balls rolled under tables or across shelves.

He glanced down at Arti, trotting along beside him like a real dog as they headed for the science module. "Too bad you're not a real dog. Rufus would've chased Thogs."

"But he might not have caught them," Arti said. "Remember the gray cat he was chasing just before I brought you here? Your dog isn't a very good hunter, I'm sorry to say. Dogs have been domesticated about twelve thousand years. Most of them have lost their wild cousins' hunting instincts."

Irritated by the AI's smug remark, he frowned. "Why are you always following me around, anyway? Maybe you should give Nan a turn!"

"She doesn't need me," Arti said.

"And I do?" he asked, surprised.

The computer-dog didn't reply.

Stung by the idea that Arti thought he needed help but Nan didn't, he began thinking up a plan of action. One day, he remembered, his dad had taken him skeet shooting. They'd had fun blasting the clay disks that rocketed up into the air, and Jerry had been good at it. "A natural," the man at the range had called him. When his mother found out where they'd been, she threw another of her fits. She didn't like Jerry learning to shoot, not even clay "pigeons." They'd never gone skeet shooting again.

But that gave him an idea.

"I could use a real weapon," he said. "Not a sling-shot like Will made. A shotgun would do."

Arti shook his head. "You won't find weapons on this station. No need for them."

"How about Edge Two?" Jerry asked. "They sometimes have to deal with problem aliens coming through, don't they? What do they use?"

The computer-dog blinked then stood absolutely still.

"Don't go into alien-overload on me!" he ordered.

Arti blinked again. "I was merely running an inventory of security weapons stored on Edge Two. Isn't that what you wished me to do?"

"You can do that? We don't have to go through Library or CenCom?" he asked. "Cool!"

"I am a very smart computer," Arti said. "You were lucky twice. One, there are a variety of weapons on Edge Two that can stun, zap, subdue, nauseate, or otherwise incapacitate enemies. And two, the shuttle was about to leave with your food supplies. I've arranged for a selection of these weapons to be loaded aboard for you. You may expect it in two hours.''

"Stun, zap, and nauseate?" Jerry repeated in disbelief. "Doesn't sound as if any of them are really lethal!"

"Of course they aren't!" Arti sounded surprised. "We don't *kill* people."

Two hours later, Jerry was standing by the airlock, unloading a crate of devices that sent low-frequency sound waves to disorient enemies, laser dazzlers to temporarily blind them, and net launchers to tangle and catch them. He stared at the packing list in dismay.

"What be this?" Will asked, coming out of the command module. He picked up a grenade launcher that came with a set of sticky stink bombs. "It looks very like an arquebus our soldiers use against Spaniards." He mimed holding the launcher like a rifle and firing it. "Go to thy watery grave, Spanish devil!"

"I think I'd trade all of this for one of your arquebuses," Jerry said. "But they're all we've got."

He armed himself with the acoustic stunner and the net launcher. Stun them first, then trap them, he hoped. Will liked the grenade launcher, but since there were no masks included to protect them from the same stink that was supposed to subdue the enemy, Jerry vetoed it. Will settled instead for the laser dazzler that looked like a long flashlight.

"Do be careful where you point that thing," Arti said. "You could disrupt my brain."

"My humble apology, shipmate," Will said. "An empty belly makes a careless man."

They set out to hunt Thogs.

Their first target rolled across the room in front of them as they entered the galley in Habitat module.

"Observe me take this enemy." Will pointed the dazzler.

Green flickering light shot out and a luminous foggy wall sprang up between the Thog and the boys.

"Oh, that's wonderful!" Jerry said sarcastically. "It can't see us, and we can't see it. A lot of use that weapon's going to be!"

"At least you're safe from counterattack," Arti murmured.

Will shut the dazzler off. The Thog had disappeared while they couldn't see it. Jerry glanced around the galley. Nan was nowhere in sight, but she'd obviously been busy making sandwiches for their supper. Four plates with bread and cheese stood in the middle of the table.

And so did another Thog, which rolled across the table past the sandwich plates. Jerry pointed the acoustic stunner and activated it. At the last minute, he remembered they had no earplugs to protect themselves if the sound was bad.

Luckily, they didn't hear the sound waves it put out. As for the Thog, it appeared to shiver like a dog shaking water off its back, then it rolled away and disappeared into the wall before he could change weapons and launch the net.

He made a quick decision and dumped the other weapon he'd brought along. If he were fast enough, he could trap Thogs in the net. He moved out of the galley and along the corridor towards the crew cabins where he'd seen Thogs this morning. Will stabbed a piece of cheese with his knife and stuffed it in his mouth, then followed Jerry. Arti went with them.

They were in luck. Opening the first door to an empty cabin, Jerry saw seven Thogs in the middle of the floor. Three more were moving along the edge by the wall. He raised the launcher and fired in one smooth, fast motion.

At the same time, the Thogs by the wall began to roll toward the others—

Too late. The net landed, trapping all ten of the Thogs—

They immediately curled around one another, rolling themselves into a ball the size of a beachball.

"I caught them!" Jerry yelled in triumph.

An odd thing happened. The net began to smoke, then the edges started to dissolve, and in a few seconds the net was entirely gone. The Thogs separated and rolled away, free.

"What happened?" he asked.

"Try again, Jerry!" Will urged.

He raised the launcher again, aimed at the one Thog that was still visible, and squeezed the trigger. It didn't work.

"Quick! Try your laser dazzler," he told Will.

Will raised the laser then frowned. "It be not working now."

"Ten of them in a ball. I should've expected it," Jerry said.

He felt stupid for not remembering, but he'd wanted to show off his skill with a gun. Thogs weren't clay pigeons. *But if I had managed to kill them,* he thought, *it wouldn't have just been pieces of clay smashed up. It would've been real living things.* The thought made him uneasy.

"Worry not," Will said. "We shall take the enemy anon."

He put an arm around Jerry's shoulder as they walked out of the Habitat module. Life seemed a lot more uncomplicated to Will than it did to him, Jerry thought.

Next morning, Jerry found DeShawn alone in the LSM studying comet data. He'd had a bad night, dreaming of chasing Thogs with Rufus. At the last minute, the Thogs turned into smelly cheese sandwiches which Rufus gulped down. No matter how many the dog ate, more kept coming. This morning, though, there were no Thogs around.

"You're just in time," DeShawn said. "Making progress?"

"None," Jerry said. "What am I in time for?"

DeShawn glanced up from the screen. "We really need the cats. I got a message from CenCom that Ailee will be back in another ten minutes."

"Do you suppose the Thogs know what they're doing to us?" he asked.

"What do you mean?" DeShawn asked.

"I'm wondering just how intelligent they are," he said.

"It's hard to see how they could have much of a brain when they don't even have a head," DeShawn said.

"I don't know. They seem to be getting smarter. Maybe it's because there are more of them."

"Something's bothering you, isn't it?" DeShawn asked.

"Yes." He hesitated, not wanting to sound like a wimp. "I guess we don't have much choice. But I don't feel right about killing something that we don't understand at all.''

"It's not healthy to feel good about any kind of killing," DeShawn agreed. Suddenly another, larger screen flushed with green light. "This is my baby, the Deep Space Telescope. Want to take a look?''

"Sure," he said. "Take my mind off Thogs."

DeShawn entered a code on a keyboard. The screen divided into two, then darkened. Then a greyish white dot glowed in the middle of one half, and a column of numbers began scrolling down the other.

"What's that? A star?'' he guessed.

DeShawn shook his head. "A comet. Luminosity enhanced so it'll show up better. It's a new one we've just discovered, about ten kilometers across. We're tracking it."

"No tail yet, of course," he said.

"No," DeShawn agreed. "That only happens when the icy ball falls close to the sun. Then the gases heat up and blow dust. And that's when they're dangerous for Earth. This one doesn't seem to be on an Earth trajectory.''

"What would you do if it were?'' he asked.

"Send a smart missile to lock onto it and explode it harmlessly out here," DeShawn explained. "Catch it before it can do any damage."

"You can do that from Oort One?"

"That's our mission." DeShawn deactivated the display. "We'd better get over to Airlock A. The shuttle should be docking soon."

Lights on the airlock panel were signaling the docking of the shuttle as Jerry and DeShawn reached it. The inner airlock door opened and Ailee stood there, surrounded by cat carriers like the ones people used to take their pets to the vet. The carriers seemed to be yowling and mewing.

"I could only get a dozen," Ailee apologized, picking up two of the carriers and stepping out. "That's all we could grow in the time."

22

"**Y**ou *grew* the cats?" Nan said later when she heard about it.

"Well, the litters had been born already," Ailee explained. "But we aged them a bit with hormones. It's too complicated to explain now."

Nan had been having visions of a laboratory with cats growing in glass jars. Yet she wasn't too bothered; the reality wasn't anywhere near as weird as some of the sci-fi movies she'd seen.

Nan, Jerry, Ailee, and Will were kneeling on the floor in the gallcy in the Habitat module, which they'd decided was the worst infested of the lot, opening crates and letting cats out. All twelve were juveniles, bigger than kittens but smaller than the adult cats they would grow to be some day.

She saw four tabbies, one smaller than the rest that reminded her of the Oak House cat, three calicos, a Persian with long white hair and blue eyes, three coal black beauties with white socks on their feet, and a tan and chocolate brown Siamese. She wanted to hug them all. She settled for stroking the little tiger-striped one.

"Miss Puss there shall prove the best, I'll wager on it," Will said.

She glanced at the dark calico cat he was pointing to. "I'll bet on the Siamese."

Will commented, "Never have I seen cat like to that one!"

"Or this tabby could be a great hunter," Nan added.

The tiger-striped tabby blinked its eyes at her. She tickled it under its chin and the tabby purred.

"I brought plenty of cat food for them too," Ailee said. "Tuna, and liver, and beef bits with bacon. All the stuff they like. But I think I'll wait to feed them till they've hunted a while."

"Beef?" Will's attention was caught by that word.

"Cat food," Ailee said firmly.

Will looked disappointed.

The cats moved around the galley, sniffing, pawing, meowing, getting to know their new home. Several of them hissed at Arti, who was lying, eyes closed, nose on paws, under the table.

"They seem to think he's a real dog," Jerry said. "Can't they tell from the smell?"

Arti opened his eyes at that.

"I meant, real dogs smell. You don't," Jerry explained.

Two of the calicos had a mock battle, hissing and batting at each other with their paws.

Ailee had also brought up a good hot stew with vegetables, beans, and rice in a vacuum box. She ladled the stew into four bowls and gave one each to Nan, Jerry, and Will. There was a new loaf of bread and a tub of butter on the table too.

"Eat while it's hot," Ailee said. "It may be the last hot food you get for a while. I'll take this one to DeShawn. Maybe I can give him a hand with the telescope."

"He'll appreciate that," Jerry said. "But what are you going to eat? I only see four bowls."

"I had enough to eat while I was in Kern!" Ailee smiled.

She went out and left them. The stew seemed to be the most delicious food Nan had ever had, but perhaps that was because she was so hungry.

"There be green things in here," Will said doubtfully, stirring his stew with his knife.

"Yup. Green peppers. Celery. Onions. Broccoli," Jerry agreed. "Great vegetable and bean stew."

"I see no meat," Will pointed out.

"I guess they forgot you were going to be sharing it." Nan laughed and cut a chunk of crusty bread which she handed to him. "They're mostly all vegetarians, you know."

"Eat if you're hungry, Will," Jerry advised. "You may not get anything else hot for a while."

"I would sooner eat Thogs!" Will exclaimed in disgust, setting down his knife.

"I wonder if we could?" she asked.

Jerry said firmly, "We're not going to try."

She didn't argue because she had no urge to taste Thog meat either. She watched as Will closed his eyes, pinched his nose with his left hand, and spooned vegetables into his mouth. She smiled. He reminded her of Ti, another boy who hated anything that was supposed to be good for him.

The cats were quiet now, all of them busy sniffing around the edges of the floor and under the table. Some had already ventured out the door. They had just barely finished eating when the little tabby she liked flushed a gray-furred Thog from its hiding place in a storage cabinet. The young cat reached its paw into the cabinet, and the Thog suddenly rolled out.

The cat gave chase across the galley floor. It looked just like the Oak House cat chasing a ball, she thought, the kind Tiger preferred with catnip inside. The Thog rolled right up to a wall and hesitated.

"Take thy prey!" Will yelled.

The cat pounced, caught the Thog between its front paws and rolled over on its back. All four paws were a blur of motion around the captured Thog.

"What's it doing?" Jerry demanded. "It's supposed to kill the Thogs, not play with them!"

"That's how cats are with mice and birds," she explained. Sometimes she wondered if Jerry even had a life, he seemed so dumb about ordinary things. Good thing she was here to balance out his nerdiness with her practicality or they wouldn't have a chance.

Will said, "Go to, my pretty, go to!"

The tiger-striped cat let go, and the Thog rolled away, the cat in hot pursuit again. Now a calico cat with beautiful tortoiseshell markings of brown and gold joined the chase, and the first cat turned to deal with this rival who dared challenge it for the interesting plaything.

Will was down on his hands and knees, trying to show the cats how it was done. "Like this! Like this, my beauties!"

Three young cats stood in a half-circle, watching him with great interest.

Then a second Thog rolled swiftly over a countertop and dropped to the floor. It whirled across the floor, past Nan's feet—which she quickly pulled up out of the way—and stopped right under the nose of the calico cat.

The young cat was so surprised she didn't react for a moment. When she did take a swipe with her paw, it was too late. The Thog had rolled away. This time it rolled over to the Thog that the tabby was using as an exercise ball.

To Nan's surprise, the second Thog rolled right up onto the cat's flashing claws with the first one. Now the little cat had difficulty because the ball had suddenly grown twice as big. His paws dropped onto his stomach with the unexpected weight; a second later, he squirmed out from under the two Thogs.

"Now what?" Jerry asked.

The tabby cat yawned and stretched as if nothing had happened, then strolled lazily out of the galley. Before Nan could say anything in defense of the cat, the Persian stalked in, a proud look in her blue eyes. Dangling from her mouth there was a Thog.

"There. See?" she said, feeling vindicated.

"Well done!" Jerry said. "That's more like it."

"Thou canst have the tidbit for thy supper, Beauty," Will said. "But for now, thou must work."

The Persian gave Will a look that seemed to express disgust with humans and Thogs both, then dropped the Thog at his feet. It twitched once, then lay still.

Nan, Jerry, and Will went out of the galley into the hall down the center of Habitat. Several Thogs rolled in all directions as if they were trying to find shelter. A black cat and another of the calicos joined forces to chase and suddenly the corridor was a muddle of spitting and hitting, fur flying and claws flashing as cats and Thogs tangled together. One thing she saw quickly: As soon as the Thogs rolled together in a ball of two or more, the cats backed off. Were they scared, she wondered, or just puzzled? And another thing, the cats spent more time fighting each other than chasing the Thogs.

By the time Ailee joined them in Habitat an hour

later, the score was still one dead Thog and nine tired but contented cats, their purrs sounding in the galley like the rumble of miniature race cars warming up at the track. None of them seemed interested in the prospect of Thogs for supper.

Three of the cats, one black, the Siamese, and the tabby that looked like the Oak House cat, had disappeared somewhere on the station.

"See how this goodly plan works?" Will said.

"How?" Jerry said. "They only killed one Thog."

"But they do seem to have scared the Thogs back into the walls," Nan said.

"And there they can't do any harm," Ailee added.

"Slow way to do it," Jerry commented.

"Not anywhere near fast enough," Nan agreed. "These kitties don't seem to have real killer instincts."

"Cats have been domesticated almost as long as dogs have, having first appeared as pets in Ancient Egypt almost thirty-seven hundred years ago," Arti said from his place under the table.

"Then the killer instinct could've gone out of cats, like it has in most dogs," Jerry said.

"That shows how little you know about cats!" Nan said heatedly. "As long as there are rats in the world, cats will hunt."

Ailee said, "Actually, we don't have rats in our world anymore. We don't even keep them in the zoo."

"Cease feeding them and they shall learn anon," Will advised.

"But that's cruel," Ailee protested.

Then DeShawn came into Habitat with something cupped in his hands. They all looked up at him.

"A huge ball of Thogs rolled past me," DeShawn

said. "Then they split up, and I saw what was making the ball so big."

He held out his hands. Nan saw the little tiger-striped cat she'd liked. It lay very still on DeShawn's dark hands.

"I think they smothered it," DeShawn said. "But, you know, I have an odd feeling this was an accident."

Ailee started to cry. Jerry put an arm around her shoulders to comfort her.

"Why do you think it was an accident?" Nan asked.

"The cat seemed to be playing with a Thog," DeShawn explained. "Then another one came along. Then another. I think it kind of snowballed until the little cat just couldn't breathe."

There they go again, she thought. These future kids didn't like to say bad things about anybody, even Thogs.

"It be the right plan e'en so." Will defended his idea. "The cats will take the victory in the end."

"If they survive long enough," Jerry said.

23

The lights flickered again, then failed. Jerry groaned. As team leader, he really had to do something about this in a hurry.

When the emergency lights took over, he stared at the dead Thog the Persian cat caught. What did these aliens eat? Nobody had seen one feeding on anything. Maybe they stole nutrients from the synthesizer, but nobody could prove that either. Whatever organs they had for sensing light must use approximately the same wavelengths as human eyes did, and they either depended on oxygen like humans, or they didn't need to breathe. He had no idea which was right. But that was the sum of their knowledge about Thogs.

Fine way to win a war when you don't know anything about the enemy, he thought. If they didn't find some answers in a hurry, they could all get killed.

He turned to DeShawn. "You have a good microscope in the SRL, don't you?"

DeShawn nodded. "What do you want to use it for?"

"It's about time someone dissected one of these Thogs. If we can learn something about alien biology, maybe we can figure out a way to disrupt it," he said.

"Let's go!" DeShawn led the way.

Jerry grabbed up the dead Thog; then he, Nan, and Ailee headed for the door. Arti trotted after them.

"Aren't you coming, Will?" Nan asked.

"Nay. I stay with the cats," Will said. "Perchance they will hunt again and I must stand ready to help."

They left him on his hands and knees with the cats.

Luckily, the science module hadn't been affected by the latest power failure and was still brightly lit. DeShawn showed Jerry the microscope, a white box with a slot and a series of dials under a computer screen.

"That's it?" Nan asked. "Doesn't look like a microscope to me! My brother had a better one in his chemistry set when he was nine. That one looks more like a toaster oven."

DeShawn looked confused for a moment. "I assure you, this is the very finest microscope available."

"There've probably been a lot of improvements since our time, Nan," Jerry explained. Nan really was hopeless with science, he thought. He turned to DeShawn. "How does it work?"

"You prepare your samples and put them on these glass slides," DeShawn said. "Then they go in this slot, and you adjust magnification and illumination with these dials so you get the best image up there on the screen. It'll analyze the chemistry of the sample for you too."

"No time to lose. Let's get to work." Jerry put the Thog on a glass board on the lab bench and looked around for a scalpel.

"Wait," Ailee said. "Maybe you'd better wear gloves, Jerry. The Thog's body fluids could be toxic to humans."

"I've got a better idea," DeShawn said. He went over to a closet on one wall and pulled out a full biohazard suit in a bright orange material. It had attached gloves and a face mask. "This'll protect you properly."

"Thanks, DeShawn."

"De nada," DeShawn replied.

Ailee helped him step into the suit and zipped up the front. He slipped his hands into the gloves and fastened them to his wrist so there were no gaps for toxic elements to reach him. He didn't think the Thogs would turn out to be poisonous, but it was better to be safe than sorry. When she lowered the mask over his head, he felt like an astronaut ready to go EVA.

Then he took the scalpel DeShawn was holding and approached the lab bench again. Everybody else stepped back a few paces behind a transparent protective barrier.

Where to start? When he'd dissected a frog in school, he'd made the first slit down the abdomen, but the Thog didn't have an obvious back or front to it. Jerry pressed it gingerly with a fingertip, feeling a bit squeamish, but he had to get over that. The Thog felt spongy, as if it didn't have a lot of bones.

"I think I'll make the first cut right here," he said, indicating a line straight along the circumference.

Even up this close, he couldn't see a mouth. How did they eat? Everything had to take in nourishment to stay alive, even Thogs. The scalpel's blade slid smoothly down through the Thog's fur. There was no blood—he was glad about that—not even any icky green stuff that might've come out of a monster in a sci-fi movie. Just as he'd suspected from pressing it, the Thog had no skeleton.

"What're you finding?" Nan wanted to know.

"No bones," he said. "That's odd. Unless the skin

acts as an exoskeleton, like a lobster. Something has to keep it all together and hold its shape."

He very carefully separated the two edges of the slit he'd made until he had the creature opened up like a book. Then he stared at the alien's internal structure. Somewhere in this gooey, yellow, jellylike mass there ought to be recognizable organs. At least a stomach, a heart, and lungs.

But he couldn't see any of them. That didn't make any sense. Maybe he was looking right at them but not recognizing them? There were some differences in the texture of the yellow goo; some of it was denser, more lumpy than the rest.

"Good thing you're wearing gloves," Nan commented. "I had a rash on my fingers and I just realized it might have come from touching a Thog."

He stopped what he was doing to stare at Nan behind the transparent barrier.

"It's almost gone now," she said. "No big deal."

Ailee said thoughtfully, "Yumiko got a little rash after touching Thogs too."

"And so did some of the others," DeShawn said. "A couple of boys showed me their hands. I didn't think it was worth worrying about. They'd been working with a cleaning fluid, and I just thought they'd been careless."

"Maybe we'll find out when I finish here," Jerry said. He'd touched the dead Thog with his bare fingers. When these gloves were off, he'd better take a look.

Ailee held out a glass slide. He noticed she'd put on another biohazard suit like the one he was wearing. He liked having her as his lab assistant.

Back to work. Carefully, he made a thin cross-section sample and laid it on the slide. Ailee took it, put it into the slot in the white box, and adjusted the dials. The wall screen lit.

"It's definitely a unicellular creature," he said. "Looks kind of like a cross-section of an amoeba."

They all stared at the image of the semicircular sample on the screen. He could see a thicker, denser membrane on the outer edge, just under the fur, and a thinner, granular jelly in the middle.

The Thogs didn't have mouths to eat or breathe, so he guessed that they took in oxygen and whatever it was they ate through their outer, fur-covered membrane. The wastes were probably excreted the same way. But they hadn't found any stuff around the ship that could be Thog droppings. Still so many puzzles. Seemed like he answered one question and that raised three more.

"Intelligence comes with complexity," Ailee said. "Having more cells means functions can be differentiated, and then you get intelligence. Maybe that's why when you get ten or more Thogs together they can make things happen to Oort One."

"Remember the Thog that reproduced when Yumiko was holding it?" Jerry said. "We didn't understand properly what happened there. Now I know. It split into two, like an amoeba. They reproduce by binary fission."

"Fine. Thanks for the biology lesson," Nan said sourly. "But what about the reason you cut this thing up in the first place? Is it poisonous?"

"Sorry," he said. He hadn't meant to show off; it was just that doing science like this excited him.

Now Ailee adjusted another dial and a long list ran up the screen on one side. They all peered at it for a moment. He saw the words hydrogen, oxygen, water, carbon dioxide—there didn't seem to be anything in the list that wasn't also found in human chemistry.

From behind the barrier, DeShawn said, "We'd better send these results to CenCom. Let the scientists on Earth analyze this stuff."

"I guess we've found why the cats wouldn't eat the Thogs," Nan said. "No self-respecting cat would eat amoebas."

"I wouldn't say this in front of Will, it might hurt his feelings," DeShawn said. "But the cat idea just isn't working out."

"At least, not fast enough," Ailee added.

"We have to do something," Jerry agreed, still gazing at the information on the screen. "Maybe we could try dogs?"

"No," Nan said. "I have a better idea."

Jerry turned to her. "What is it?"

"I think we should bring up a saber-toothed tiger," Nan said.

"Smilodon californicus?" Ailee said. "But, Nan, they're way too dangerous!"

"And the ones in our zoo are full grown," DeShawn said. "Neither one of them would survive t-porting."

"I don't mean the parents," Nan said. "I mean we should bring up the cub the female was expecting when we saw her. She must've had it by now."

For the first time in over an hour, Arti spoke up. "A small, healthy male. This is the first cub to be born naturally."

"We'll need to do whatever Ailee did with the kittens to make that cub grow big enough to hunt, but not enough to be hurt t-porting," Nan said.

"You can't train a cat the way you train a dog," Jerry objected.

"This isn't a cat, it's a tiger," Nan replied.

She was never going to get that one right, he thought. He tried something else. "Anyway, they're dangerous from birth."

"We don't know that yet," Arti put in. "Remember, the other two were cloned from DNA."

"Whose side are you on?" Jerry asked the AI.

Ailee said, "Doctor Pike won't like this!"

"The reason they brought us here is because they don't have any better ideas," Nan argued. "I'll take Will with me."

"Okay then," Jerry said reluctantly, picturing the enormous dagger teeth on the beast in the extinct animals zoo. "We'll try your plan. When do you want to leave?"

"How about right away?" Nan said.

Nan left the science module and went to find Will. She needed to get moving again, do something active.

The automatic safety doors of the transfer node sighed shut behind her and she was in Habitat. She walked as quickly as she could without losing her balance and thought about the problem.

If you had a cat or a dog, you could figure out what it was likely to do by knowing how cats or dogs reacted to something. Maybe your new cat had never seen a bird before, but you could be pretty sure it would pounce if it had the chance because that's what cats do. Just like Jerry should've known that if his dog was off the leash when a stray cat ran past, its instinct to hunt prey would be triggered and it would give chase.

The emergency lights were still on in Habitat when she arrived. By their lower glow, she saw Will lying on his side on his bunk, clutching his knees. Two cats sat with him. He didn't look up.

"What's the matter?" she asked.

"I know not," he said in a small voice. "It seems the devil hath lit a fire in my gut."

"You're in pain?"

He nodded and immediately made a face. "My head burns also."

Worried now, she came into the room and put her hand on Will's forehead. He was very hot to her touch. Stomachache, fever, what could that mean?

"Have you spoken to the medibot?" she asked.

"Nay, I trust not the talking boxes." He sat part way up and tried to smile at her, but she thought that made him look worse.

"Well I'm going to call it," she said. "Lie back down."

The cats didn't bother to shift position as Will moved. I could've predicted that, she thought. Cats seem to know when you aren't feeling well, and they stay with you.

She quickly crossed the hall to her cabin and went to the terminal on Ailee's desk; she keyed in a call for the medical robot. It would be very bad news if Will were to get sick right now. They'd have to delay their trip to Kern, or she'd have to go without him to train a saber-toothed tiger. Neither of those choices appealed to her.

The medibot arrived quickly and rolled into Will's small cabin. Unlike the other 'bots that weren't specialized, this one looked like a medicine chest on wheels with a stethoscope permanently attached to one "arm" extension. She stood in the doorway, trying not to get in the way, as the 'bot examined the boy and asked questions about his symptoms.

While she waited for the 'bot's diagnosis, she thought about the Thogs again. The theory behind the "hive mind" said that even if individual creatures— or aliens—had very limited amounts of brain cells, when you put them all together into a big clump, you'd get enough brain cells to allow intelligent behavior.

She watched the medibot give Will an injection. The boy closed his eyes, but he didn't complain. His color hadn't come back yet; his cheeks were usually so rosy that it was odd to see them pale like this.

The Thogs had only one cell in their entire bodies, she thought. So how could multiplying them produce intelligence? A million times zilch was still zilch. Yet clumps of Thogs could cause dangerous things to happen to the space station. What were they trying to do? Or could you even say they were "trying to do" anything at all? Were they just somehow blindly messing things up for humans, like they'd killed the little cat?

The medibot was done. It rolled backward out of Will's cabin, then reversed itself. She stepped into its path.

"Is Will going to be all right?" she asked.

"He has an upset stomach," the 'bot's tinny voice said. "Mild food poisoning. Something he ate."

"But we've all been eating the same things."

"Your friend found another source of food," the 'bot said. It trundled away without explaining.

She crossed the hall into his cabin. "Will? What have you been up to?"

"The talking box assures me I shall live," he said, giving her a weak smile. "But the pain hath not left me."

"The 'bot gave you something for it," she said. "Give it time to work."

He looked serious again. "Nan, I trust not the talking boxes. They bring to my mind the Spaniard in his coat of steel, and the Spaniard lies in his teeth! I suffer greatly from the diarie. I fear the bloody flux, Nan. Think you it be so?"

"I've never heard of it," she said. "I doubt you have it anyway. The 'bot said it was something you ate. What did you eat that the rest of us didn't?"

"But it was beef, Nan," he said in a small voice. "I craved meat so."

Incredulous, she stared at him. "You ate *cat food*?" Even a little kid knew not to eat pet food! But in Will's time there was no such thing as special meals for cats or dogs; how was he to know cat food wasn't fit for human consumption? "No wonder you have diarrhea!"

Will dislodged the cats from his lap and stood up. He said in a proud tone, "Thy scorn hath disturbed my sickbed. I shall rise and serve though I be dying."

She laughed. "Gimme a break, Will! You'll survive. But I need you to get up and get dressed. We're going back to Kern to fetch a very large cat."

While he was still grumbling about his stomach cramps, she went back to her cabin. The disease Will thought he'd had intrigued her. What if it were dangerous and the medibot had missed diagnosing it? She sat at the desk and keyed in the commands to raise Library.

"Hello, Nan," Library's warm male voice said. "How can I help you today?"

"Have you heard of an Elizabethan disease called 'bloody flux?' " she asked. "Is it serious?"

"Oh, yes indeed," Library said. "It's an old name for one of two types of dysentery. The symptoms are diarrhea with blood in the stools, cramps, and fever. But you aren't at risk for dysentery here, Nan. The infection is spread in filthy environments by houseflies that feed on contaminated food and excrement."

"You said two types?"

"Bacillary, caused by bacteria," Library said.

"And amoebic, caused by amoebas. Before the discovery of antibiotics, either type could be fatal."

"Amoebas?" It was slowly beginning to click into place in her mind.

"The human alimentary tract can be home to six kinds of parasitic amoeba," Library said. "The *Entamoeba histolytica* causes dysentery—"

"Wait!" she ordered. "This is more than I want to know right now. But let me get this straight. Amoebas are microscopic creatures, right? And yet you're saying they can kill a person?"

"If the invasion is left untreated," Library agreed.

She thought about that for a moment. "Yet if the patient dies, the amoebas are out of luck, aren't they? They perish too."

"Correct," Library said. "Many if not most parasites in nature have learned to be symbionts, coexisting with their human or animal hosts so they can reproduce and pass on their genes. Usually, the host animal benefits from the parasite too. For instance, humans have many kinds of benevolent parasites in their alimentary tract helping the digestive process. But some disease-causing ones don't seem to have learned that useful trick."

She shuddered. "One more thing. If the Thogs are somehow like the good kind of amoeba, then they need us, but they could accidentally kill us and themselves too, right?"

"Unicellular creatures are not highly evolved," Library explained. "We should expect a lot of random and self-defeating behavior. And that of course is dangerous because it's difficult to predict."

"Thanks, Library," she said. "You've given me a lot to think about."

When she turned away from the desk she found Will standing in the door.

"The potion hath worked," he announced. "I shall not die yet. Tell me of this very large cat we go to find. I tire of this metal galleon."

She grinned at him. "We're going to fetch a saber-toothed tiger. And you'd better keep your hands off its food!"

25

Jerry watched as the shuttle carrying Nan and Will to Edge Two separated from the space station. There were no windows on Oort One, so he had to watch this on a video screen mounted above a computer in the command module. DeShawn stood behind him, sorting though a box of program disks and cubes. With no help left on the station now that all the kids had been sent home, DeShawn did the little chores as well as the big ones like monitoring the comet watch.

He had an odd feeling, watching Nan leave. They'd been in this together from the first moment when she saved him from the gang members. Right from the beginning, he'd known she would be useful on the team; that was why he'd stood up for her when bad-tempered Doctor Pike wanted to send her back. Since then, she'd become more than just someone from his own century. Even though she could be irritating and bossy, he was going to miss her company and her help. It might be several days before she came back, and a lot could happen up here in several days.

Then the video screen went blank.

"Oh no!" DeShawn exclaimed.

Jerry turned. "What happened?"

The control center had a row of computers. They

were all as blank as the one he'd been watching.

"The computers just crashed," DeShawn said. "All of them! This is very bad news."

"I can see that," he agreed. "But the lights are still working. How come?"

"We have lighting and computers on separate systems for a reason," DeShawn said.

Jerry thought for a moment. "What if some rogue comet chooses now—when we're as good as blind—to head for Earth?"

"More than that," DeShawn said gloomily. "The computers monitor all the automatic systems on Oort One. Without them, we won't know if something is going seriously wrong until it's too late."

Jerry tried to be more optimistic than he felt. "Let's wait a while before we panic, DeShawn. Everything else the Thogs have knocked out has eventually begun working again. Most things are okay after about five minutes."

DeShawn said, "Like the food synthesizer, I suppose!"

Ailee came into the command center. "The cats are still chasing Thogs into the walls, and we're still getting the occasional one in the traps, but it's much too slow."

Jerry was thoughtful. He couldn't see how an amoebalike creature could have any intelligence at all. He couldn't see the answer yet.

"There's a lot more of them now too," Ailee said. "They're reproducing fast. I'm starting to wish Will had taught us how to use a slingshot after all. 'The best Thogs be dead Thogs!' as Will says."

That made Jerry remember he'd touched the dead Thog yesterday with his bare hands. He stared down at his hands, turning them, palms up. Sure enough, there was a red patch running across the fingers where he'd held the Thog. It didn't hurt, and it didn't look serious. But what did it mean? It could be some kind of mild allergic reaction. Later, if he remembered about it, he'd ask Library about allergies and what triggered them.

The three of them sat and stared at each other. Maybe the computers would start working again eventually or maybe not. All they could do was wait and see. It was very quiet in the command center. The space station was a really creepy place to be when there were almost no people on it. Oort One wasn't a big station, but right now it seemed enormous and spooky. Jerry was glad the lights were still working.

He looked at his watch. Five minutes had gone by and the computer screens were still dark and lifeless.

"Maybe the numbers have something to do with it," he suggested. "The Thogs may have reached critical mass. It's sort of like a nuclear reaction. That's when the explosion happens."

"Do you really think they could explode?" Ailee asked.

Jerry shrugged. "No. I was just borrowing a term." Then he had second thoughts. "But we don't really know, do we?"

"If we don't get the computers back on-line, the shuttle won't be able to dock if it comes back pilotless as it usually does," DeShawn pointed out. "It relies on programmed instructions from the computer to line itself up with the airlock. Without them, it could crash into the side of the station, damaging itself and us."

"That happened to the Russian space station *Mir,* I remember," Jerry said. "Could be a serious problem."

He timed another five minutes by his watch as they

waited for something to happen. Nothing did.

"What're we going to do now?" DeShawn asked.

Privately, Jerry thought this was a crazy way to build a space station. Everything was dependent on the computers and there seemed to be no emergency backup plans. Once again, he saw clearly what a problem it was for the people of DeShawn and Ailee's century, where everything was always so perfect. When something finally did go wrong, they weren't prepared to deal with it. No wonder they needed kids from his own mixed up and imperfect time, kids who were good at thinking up unusual solutions to awkward problems!

"Thinking of computers," he said, "has anybody seen Arti lately?"

"The AI was in Habitat when I left," Ailee said. "Looking at Thogs—Oh no!"

Jerry jumped up from his chair and headed out of the command module. Arti was a computer too, a special one. Could the Thogs damage him, put him out of business like the ones in the control center? Arti was only an artificial dog, but Jerry had grown fond of him.

He walked as fast as he could without losing his balance in the low gravity. As he entered the Habitat module, Ailee was right behind him.

Arti was standing like a statue of a dog in the middle of the galley. Not a hair on his coat moved, and his steel eyes had a glazed-over look to them.

"Arti!" Jerry yelled.

Ailee pointed to something under the table. "Look."

In the shadow under the long galley table, Jerry saw a large furry ball. Thogs. At least two dozen of them, he guessed. Enough to damage Oort One's computers? Enough to scuttle Arti, at least.

"Can you reactivate him, the way you did last time?" he asked.

"Not if the Thogs have damaged the circuits in his head," Ailee replied.

He was staring at the ball of Thogs, wondering what to do, when suddenly it fell apart. Thogs rolled quickly away in all directions.

Arti blinked, shook himself, and opened his mouth. "That was most interesting. I hadn't had a chance to observe a large group interaction of Thogs before."

"Alien overload," Ailee groaned. "We thought you were damaged."

"Certainly not," Arti said. "But I found out that the aliens actually seem to develop some form of mind, or at least mental ability, when they're combined."

"We've figured that out already!" Jerry interrupted, annoyed with Arti for the worry he'd caused them.

"Have you now?" Arti said, gazing at Jerry. "What else have you figured out?"

"You're a computer," he said. "But you're still functioning when the station's computers aren't."

"Correction. I'm an artificial intelligence. Much more than your average computer."

"Yes. And the difference keeps you working," Jerry said. "Question is, can you patch in and run things if we need you to?"

"The whole station?" Arti asked, tilting his head to one side. "That's a tall order."

A single gray Thog rolled lazily across the galley floor past Jerry's feet as if it had as much right to be there as the humans did.

"They act like they own the station now," Ailee said gloomily.

"Unless patching Arti in works, nobody can get on the station," Jerry said. "And we can't get off. We're prisoners of the Thogs."

"Then I suggest you'd better make a start on using me to find a solution," Arti said.

The three of them headed back to the command module.

26

"**W**ait! I have need of the jakes," Will said, pointing to the universal sign for a restroom.

They were on Edge Two where the shuttle from the space station had just brought them. All around them, colorfully dressed teenagers hurried to and fro on errands.

Nan glanced at him. "Are you sure this is really necessary?"

"Aye," Will said, nodding. "By my troth, I swear it."

Will found modern toilets fascinating. He'd told her they had nothing like them in the sixteenth century. Even kings and queens used a hole in a corner of the castle wall that went all the way to the ground, and they thought they were lucky not to have to squat over an open sewer. On Drake's ship, he'd told her, the "jakes" was on the bow, straight over the ocean, a very unpleasant place in bad weather.

But then she remembered his upset stomach just a few hours ago. This trip was probably for real.

"Hurry up then," she said.

Will disappeared. As she waited, she watched the Edge Two kids come and go, most of them not much older than seventeen. The adults up here wouldn't be going home any day soon if they ever went home at all. She thought they must consider their work very important to make such a sacrifice.

A door to one of the offices around the central hall opened and a tall man came out. She glanced curiously at him and her blood ran cold.

It was Doctor Arlo Pike.

But it couldn't be! There was no way he could've come this far through the t-ports without frying his brains. Even Pike wasn't crazy enough to do a thing like that. He must've come up the slow way, by ship, yet that didn't make sense either. She didn't know how long it took to get from Earth to Edge Two in the Oort Cloud the slow way, but it had to be *years*. There hadn't been enough time.

Yet she couldn't forget Pike's thin face and constant scowling expression as if he'd bitten into a sour lemon. And there it was.

The man had stopped to talk to a girl about Nan's age. Nan hid in a doorway across from him and watched. They seemed to be having some sort of argument; the girl had given him something and he didn't seem happy with it. He was frowning and waving his arms. The girl shrugged and walked off.

That was how Pike behaved all right, she thought. What could he possibly be doing up here? What was important enough to him that he'd take such a risk to get here? Then she remembered what he'd said to her: "The minute you do something stupid, I'm going to send you right back." Arlo Pike had risked his own life to keep an eye on Nan Smith.

He had to be absolutely crazy! For the first time since she'd met him, she actually felt scared of him. But she wasn't scared enough to give up her plan.

Just then, Will came out of the restroom, grinning

as if he'd been on a trip to his own private Disneyland. She put her finger to her lips, afraid he'd attract Pike's attention. Luckily, the man was about to enter the office he'd come out of a moment ago. She waited until the door closed behind him.

"Did you see who that was?" she asked.

"Nay. Who?" Will said.

"Arlo Pike," she said. "Quick, we'd better go through the portal as fast as we can!"

She took Will's arm and pushed him into the t-port booth.

"I never forget the face of mine enemy," Will said, glancing over his shoulder. "Even Spanish pirates who all look most remarkably alike. But I think you be in error this time, Nan."

"No error!" she said grimly.

When they arrived on Earth, bright sunshine and fresh, flower-scented air met them. It felt good to have the real, solid ground of a planet underfoot again. Nan realized how much she'd miss Earth if she had to spend her life on a space station. Even the worst day at Oak House was better than permanent exile in that blackness.

And setting foot on Earth again drove away the idea that she could've possibly glimpsed Arlo Pike on Edge Two. *Just my active imagination,* she thought. *Maybe something about being in outer space too long makes you start hallucinating.*

Doctor Serena Cee was there to meet them. She hugged Will first and then Nan. Nan saw the big silly grin on Will's face and was disgusted.

"Welcome back," Doctor Cee said. "We're glad to see you, but we're also terribly worried about what's going on up there. The situation seems to be worsening. Communications are down now."

"Worry not, my lady," Will said, making a deep bow to Doctor Cee. "We shall defeat your enemies and save you."

Oh, please! Nan thought. Out loud she said, "The new plan's going to work. I know it is. But we should get started as soon as possible."

"Certainly," Doctor Cee said. "I must admit, your request startled us. We wouldn't ever have imagined using a smilodon cub! Yet that's why we brought you here, to think of the things we missed, isn't it?"

"Did you have time to analyze Jerry's dissection data?" Nan asked.

The scientist nodded. "Come along. I'll explain everything."

Doctor Cee led them to a waiting aircar. Nobody said much on the journey over to the zoo. Even Will was silent, but Nan noticed that he kept glancing at Doctor Cee when he thought she wasn't looking. The poor kid had a bad crush on the pretty scientist, she thought.

At the zoo, they hurried past the pterodactyls and the dodo birds and came to the smilodon quarters. They passed that too and stopped at a low building with no windows and a flat roof.

"We've already separated the cub from his mother," Doctor Cee said. "He's here, in the nursery."

Doctor Cee opened the door and led them inside a warm building with glass-fronted cages on either side of a long corridor and soft, even light pouring down from a skylight. Doctor Cee indicated a door beside the next window and they went through into the cage. The plate over the door said SMILODON CALIFORNICUS. It was darker in here, to protect the baby smilodon's immature eyes, and Nan couldn't see the cub at first.

"Do you want to hold him?" Doctor Cee asked.

Nan nodded and held out her arms. Doctor Cee bent over and lifted something which she carefully placed in Nan's arms.

Nan looked down at the tiny animal asleep in her arms. It looked like a very young kitten, but bigger, about the size of a full grown cat. Then it yawned, revealing rows of sharp little teeth, and she saw the buds on either side of its upper jaw that would later grow into the huge tusks that gave the adult its name. Like human babies, it had "milk teeth" for the time being, smaller ones that wouldn't get in the way when the cub was nursing.

The little cub opened amber eyes and gazed up at her. She felt a wave of tenderness sweep over her; it looked so soft and vulnerable.

"Hello, Smiley," she said. "You're going on a big adventure for such a little guy."

"How long, think you, to grow him quickly large?" Will asked.

"We don't know for sure," Doctor Cee admitted. "Every animal is different in the way it reacts to the accelerated growth hormones that we're going to use. And we don't usually try to work this fast."

Nan stroked the cub's soft head. "I think we should aim to grow him a little bit, then stop and train him. Do that over and over until he's big enough to fight Thogs."

"How big must that be?" Will asked.

"I figure when he's about the size of a Saint Bernard," she said. Then seeing Will's puzzled expression, she translated. "A very big dog!"

"We're quite excited about your idea, Nan," Doctor Cee said.

Nan nodded. It did seem now that she'd overreacted on Edge Two. Nobody wanted her off the team, probably not even Doctor Pike. He was grumpy, but she didn't think he was stupid enough to sabotage the only chance they had to get rid of the Thogs. Certainly he wasn't dumb enough to risk his life to spy on her.

"By the way," she said. "Where's Doctor Pike?"

"Arlo's not here," Doctor Cee said. "He went out of town on private business."

Nan felt as if she'd fallen through a hole into an icy lake.

27

Jerry and Ailee squatted on the floor of the control center in the command module, watching DeShawn help Arti patch in to the antenna controls. In a corner, one of the 'bots sat uselessly, disabled by the Thogs. Jerry yawned and shook his head, trying to stay alert. This was their third day of trying, having things work for a few moments, maybe an hour or two, then crash once more.

He yawned again. I'd better be careful, he thought; accidents are more likely to happen when you're tired. He forced himself to concentrate on what Ailee and DeShawn were doing.

"Give me a hand here, Jerry," DeShawn said, pointing to some wires he wanted Jerry to hold.

It was a sight none of Jerry's old friends would ever have believed. The dog that looked so much like Rufus had a flap open on the back of his head, just behind one ear. Wires came out of it and DeShawn was attaching them to a panel under one of the computers.

"There," DeShawn said, sitting back on his heels. "Try that, Arti."

Jerry stared up at the blank screen over the computer. There was silence for a moment. Nothing happened.

DeShawn sighed. "I'll try a different arrangement."

"How're you deciding what to hook up where?" he asked.

"Guesswork," DeShawn replied. "I've run through the repair manuals and you know how much luck I've had. Nada."

"Maybe if you took Arti's main nerve cable, then bypassed the central unit, patched it directly into the transmitter . . ." he suggested.

DeShawn stared at him. Jerry shrugged. He knew what DeShawn was too polite to say: *What can you possibly know about artificial intelligence?*

But Arti said, "It's worth a try, you know."

The computer-dog winked at Jerry.

"Okay." DeShawn leaned forward again, peering into the AI's exposed cyberbrain.

Jerry watched intently as DeShawn rearranged cables, plugging and unplugging. These complicated future machines seemed to use fewer cables than his own home computer used to run the monitor, the keyboard, the CD-ROM, and the printer.

Then, still crouching on his heels, DeShawn scuttled over to the computer's control panel and repeated the process.

"Ready now," DeShawn said.

Once again the three of them stared at the screen. Nothing.

"I can't think of anything else to try," DeShawn said. "If this—"

"Wait," Arti interrupted. "I'm sensing something from the low-gain antenna."

In the silence, Jerry could hear his own heart beating faster than normal. If Arti couldn't fix the directional antenna they were in big trouble. And if the AI couldn't do it, they didn't have any other options.

The screen on the wall over the main computer broke up into streaks of a dull silver color. Black wavy lines ran over it, then disappeared. He held his breath. The silver blinked out and the screen was blank once again.

"It was a start, Arti," Ailee said. "You almost did it."

"But almost isn't good enough," Jerry said. "Why is this taking so long?"

Ailee looked surprised that he would be so rude. He shrugged; it was the sort of thing Nan might've said, but he was feeling uptight like he did sometimes before a physics or mathematics exam where he wanted to do his best.

"There's more than one antenna and radar dish on two different booms," Arti explained. "I have to eliminate them one by one till I find the culprit."

"I knew that," Jerry said. "I shouldn't have complained. I'm tired and grumpy."

"Understandable. But at least I've figured out the problem this time," Arti said. "The last Thog power surge locked one particular antenna in position. And it's not right for any of our purposes."

"What're we going to do?" Jerry asked. "Can't we fix it?"

"Not from in here," Arti said.

"I could go outside," Ailee suggested.

"Too dangerous!" DeShawn objected quickly.

Jerry asked, "Are you thinking of going EVA, Ailee?"

"Yes," she said.

Extravehicular activity meant going outside the space station in a special space suit to make repairs, he knew; even in his time astronauts did it on shuttle missions. But he also knew it was still dangerous. The vacuum of space was unforgiving if you made just a little mistake. He was impressed with how brave Ailee was to volunteer. But with the Thogs around, messing things up . . . he didn't want to think about the possibilities.

"Sounds too dangerous to me too," he said.

"We don't have a choice," Ailee argued. "Someone has to go outside."

"Then I'll do it!" DeShawn said.

"But I'm the one who's trained for emergency repairs on the skin, you know," Ailee objected.

"I don't want you to take the risk," DeShawn said.

Jerry looked from one to the other. This was the closest he'd ever heard any of the people of the future come to an argument. It made them suddenly seem more real to him.

"Maybe DeShawn's right," he said. "It doesn't sound like a good idea."

Ailee touched his arm and smiled. "Thanks, Jerry. But I know what I'm doing."

She disappeared quickly out of the control center as if she thought Jerry would try to talk her out of it if she stayed. DeShawn looked glum; he moved over to a storage locker at the base of one of the curving walls of the command module.

"This is where we keep equipment to use when someone's on EVA," DeShawn said to him. "Since I can't change her mind, I'd better take care of this while you help Ailee suit up. She'll be over by Airlock B. I'll meet you both there."

Jerry had never noticed Airlock B. Airlock A was the big one near the command module where the little shuttle bringing them here had docked.

Arti saw his hesitation. "B's at the aft end of the

connector, near the science module. It's a small airlock for personnel egress only.''

"Right," Jerry said, trying to guess which was fore and which was aft on a rotating space station. He had serious doubts about this latest plan, but what alternative did they have? And Ailee said she'd been trained to do it. He walked as quickly as he dared out of Command and down the connecting corridor toward the SRL.

When he knew what he was looking for, Airlock B was easy to find. It was at the other end of the connector to Airlock A. Ailee was in the lock already with the inner doors open, wriggling her way into a space suit.

"Give me a hand with these straps," she said.

She was already wearing a kind of skintight jumpsuit which he guessed was designed to cool and ventilate under the space suit itself. He'd studied the manuals for NASA's space flights and knew all about an astronaut's need to breathe pure oxygen and flush nitrogen out of her body before going on EVA. She stepped into the bottom half of the waiting space suit, legs first, then held out her arms for him to help her into the top half.

For a moment Jerry felt envious of Ailee. He'd always dreamed of being an astronaut, but his mom wouldn't even hear of him going to Space Camp in Alabama. Then he remembered what an amazing adventure he was actually on, and he let go of envy altogether. There was simply no need for it.

"With the computers not working, how are we going to know what's happening to you out there?" he asked. It would be nail-biting time if they had to wait in ignorance until she came back, unable to see or hear from her.

Ailee pressed a small square box onto her chest, where it adhered. "Communications carrier," she said. "Including a vidcam. It bypasses the main computer system and sends a signal the AI can pick up."

"I'm sure glad to hear that!" he said.

Ailee grinned. "I'm almost ready. The tether's on that wall. It's also the umbilical that carries all the data and communications. It unreels as I move away from the airlock."

"Umm," he said. "In my time, astronauts need something called an EMU, Extravehicular Mobility Unit. It's a big old thing with arms like an armchair for maneuvering around in space. But I don't see one here."

"That was a long time ago, Jerry," she said gently. "We do things differently now."

He felt the hot blood rush into his cheeks. *Idiot!* he thought. What would she think of him? That was certainly not the way to impress a girl. He must've sounded like Will telling one of his tales about how things were done on the *Golden Hind.*

Ailee slipped the helmet over her hair and snapped it to the rest of her space suit. There was a lamp built in at the top, something like the lamp in a firefighter's helmet. She was going to need the light because it was dark out where she was headed. She smiled at him again through the face plate, blue eyes sparkling. Jerry felt a stab of fear for her. She was going to risk her life out in space.

"Be careful, Ailee. It's dangerous out there."

That was another dumb comment, he thought as soon as he'd said it. He was disgusted with himself for turning into such a dork. But he liked Ailee; she was smart and she was kind, and it didn't hurt that her hair smelled like apples, his favorite fruit. In fact he liked her a lot. And that was another dumb thing for him to do.

"Thanks for worrying, Jerry," she said. "I'll be okay."

DeShawn appeared with the emergency communications equipment and suddenly the moment had arrived.

The two boys stepped back out of the airlock and closed the door. This one had a manually operated door lock, and didn't rely on computer control like Airlock A. DeShawn turned a big wheel and the inner doors of the airlock sealed. A red light came on; the oxygen in the lock was being pumped out.

Then a second red light lit, signaling the opening of the outer doors and the emptying of Airlock B.

Ailee had stepped out into space.

28

"**Y**ou have visitors, Nan," Doctor Serena Cee said.

Nan was standing by the lab building, waiting for one of the 'bots to bring Smiley out for a training session. Will had gone off in search of a snack. She was amused by the Elizabethan boy. The food shortage he'd been through on Oort One seemed to have convinced him famines could occur even in the future. As a result he was determined not to get caught without a full stomach.

Doctor Cee beckoned to a tall couple. "Lewis and Philomena Sig Gan would like to meet you. They're DeShawn's parents."

Nan shook the hands DeShawn's parents held out. She saw that DeShawn had the same rich coffee-color skin as his mother, but he had his dad's wide, friendly smile. She said, "Pleased to meet you. DeShawn's a good kid."

"We want to express our appreciation to you for helping us," Lewis Gan said.

"De nada," Nan said, which was something she'd often heard DeShawn say, and the parents both smiled.

"I speak for the parents of all the kids on the station when I say we'd have rather been up there ourselves," the mother said. "We can't thank you enough."

For the first time since she could remember, Nan felt tongue-tied. They all shook hands again and the Gans walked away.

"Nice people," she said.

"They are indeed," Doctor Cee said. "DeShawn is their second child to serve on Oort One. His older sister came back just a few months before DeShawn went up. Every member of that family is either an astronomer or an astrophysicist."

Doctor Cee looked thoughtful. "I didn't tell them we seem to have lost contact with Oort One again. I have to assume that it'll be only temporary this time too."

"Thogs," Nan said. "But we're gonna get 'em!"

"The AI that went up with you should be able to solve the latest communications problem," Doctor Cee said. But we'll send up a new comm unit when you return, just in case."

The door to the lab building opened and a 'bot trundled out, followed by what looked like a Labrador retriever puppy with short, golden fur, stubby legs, and a thick, muscular neck.

"Yo, Smiley!" she said. "You're getting to be a big boy!"

The smilodon cub bounded over to her and jumped, planting huge front paws on her chest and almost knocking her backward under its weight. Close up, she could see the saber teeth that were buds a little while ago; now they were already a couple of inches long. The cub tried to lick her face. Laughing, she pushed him gently down.

Library had estimated that a smilodon cub would normally be an adult in about a year. Since this was the first one born naturally, nobody could be certain; the two that were cloned from DNA were not good examples. Nan figured an eight- to nine-month old cub would be about right to hunt Thogs.

The veterinary scientists on the staff carefully computed how much accelerated growth hormone to give Smiley and at what intervals. They had arranged it so that the cub's mealtimes were always accompanied by images and smells of Thogs, so that he would associate food with the aliens. In between, Nan cuddled him and played with him, getting him used to her.

The 'bot handed Nan a wrapped package of meat she used as a treat when Smiley did a good job of learning what she taught him. She put it in her pocket. The cub lifted his head and scented the meat. He nosed against her pocket.

"Not just yet," she said. "You have to earn it."

Smiley turned his attention to trying to chew her shoes. She patted him; he responded by nibbling playfully on her ankle.

"Ouch!" she said. "That hurt. Your new teeth are sharp."

Doctor Cee looked thoughtful. "You aren't going to have much time with Smiley. He's going to be too powerful and dangerous in a very short time. We gave him a nannie that should produce an aversion to attacking humans, but we're not sure how well it will work. And we've never tried aging an animal this size so fast before. It could have some unforeseen side effects."

"Such as?" Nan asked.

"That's what we don't know. But rapid growth could affect his temper. You must be very careful at all times, Nan."

"I intend to," she said.

She threw a ball for Smiley to retrieve, a gray furry one the size of a Thog. When he did as he was told, she rewarded him with a cube of meat.

"Good boy, Smiley," she said each time. "You're the best!"

Will and the 'bot carrying Smiley's lunch appeared at the same time. The tiger cub stood with its front feet in the huge bowl, gulping down the food.

Will gazed at the cub then up at Doctor Cee. "He be much grown since last I saw him. Perchance if there were more meat in my victuals and less green things, I too would grow quickly tall?"

Doctor Cee laughed. "Nice try, Will! But if you grew up too fast, you couldn't go back to Oort One."

Will gave her a sly smile.

"Why can't adults t-port long distances?" Nan asked. "Is it to do with weight? Or brain power?"

"Doctor Pike thinks it's growth that matters," Doctor Cee said. "As long as a living being, human or animal, is still growing, t-porting is safe."

Serena Cee's words brought back Nan's worries about Doctor Pike. He hadn't been around since they'd arrived on Earth, so she was certain now that she'd been right and had seen him on Edge Two. Pike was taking an enormous risk with his own health to follow Nan into space to check up on her. She was shaken to think that somebody could dislike her that much. What had she ever done to deserve it?

The cub had just overturned the food dish and was standing on it. Another 'bot came toward them, holding a leather harness in one appendage and a leash in another.

"Back to work, Smiley," Nan said.

"Smiley's going to be harder to handle pretty soon," Doctor Cee explained. "Better he gets used to a harness now than later when he's stronger."

"I'll put it on him," Nan said. "Come here, Smiley boy."

The cub allowed her to fasten the harness around his body quietly enough, but as soon as she attached the leash and he felt the tension he began to tug. Already he was strong enough that he could jerk Nan all over the lawn as she tried to teach him to walk with her. Catching her foot in a tuft of longer grass at one point, she sat down with a bump. Smiley immediately climbed in her lap and tried to lick her face again. Up close, his fur had a sweet clover smell.

She gave the cub a lump of meat. "You're the best, Smiley," she said, handing the leash to the 'bot to take the cub back to the lab building. "Don't want to make him hate working with us," she said.

Next morning, the three of them stood on the lawn by the lab again, waiting for Smiley to emerge; one of the veterinarians from the zoo who monitored Smiley's development joined them.

A cub almost as big as a Saint Bernard came out, with dagger teeth that were now about four inches long, half as long as they would be at full length. He was much bigger than the 'bot who led him.

The veterinarian stepped forward and passed a small thin wallet-sized metal device over the smilodon's chest and haunches. Smiley shook himself impatiently and tried to pull away. The vet read his results for a moment.

"He's healthy," the vet said. "And I don't think you'd better wait too much longer, or you won't be able to control him at all. You may even have trouble now."

Will stood up from where he'd been sitting on the

lawn and dusted grass off his blue jumpsuit. "Ready at thy command, Lady Nan."

But his face had gone white, Nan noticed. He was scared of working with Smiley. She had to admit she was a bit surprised herself at how big Smiley was; he came up to her waist this time. As she took the leash from the 'bot, Smiley rubbed against her leg, and she could hear the rumble of a purr deep in his throat.

"He has obviously bonded with you, Nan," Doctor Cee said. "That's a good sign."

"I understand him," she said.

"But please don't take any chances," Doctor Cee added. "Never forget you have a wild animal there."

"Hard to forget such daggers, methinks," Will commented.

"We analyzed the Thog Jerry dissected," Doctor Cee said. "We found that the Thogs' amino acids, the building blocks of the peptides and proteins, are right-handed. Just about every organism on Earth, including humans and Smiley, makes or uses left-handed ones."

Will interrupted, "The Thog hath no hands!"

Serena Cee smiled at him. "That's right, Will. But this term comes from something chemists do with the molecules under polarized light. So no matter how many Thogs Smiley eats, his body won't be able to process any of them. They won't harm him, but they won't feed him either."

"Then he'll still need his regular meals," Nan said.

"He's up to five pounds of meat a day," the vet said. "And that'll go up. But we've made a special vitamin and nutrition supplement in case he feels too full of Thogs to eat real food."

"Okay." Nan nodded. "I understand that."

"We know the Thogs are in Oort One's walls, and we need time to think of a way to get rid of them,"

Doctor Cee added. "But while they're in the walls, they can't form large balls, so they can't do much damage. Even if Smiley doesn't catch any Thogs but manages to scare them out of sight, he'll be useful."

The vet said, "I'm giving you a tranquilizer for him, just in case you have any trouble. It should knock him out instantly."

"Report to us as soon as you can," Doctor Cee said.

Nan and Smiley entered the t-port booth after Will. As the door closed behind them, Smiley growled.

29

DeShawn had found a portable vidscreen, much smaller than the wall-mounted ones in the control center. The two boys and Arti sat on the floor in the SRL, watching it now as Ailee began her slow climb up the side of the station to reach the malfunctioning antenna. The AI had the flap open behind his ears again.

This equipment didn't seem up to the advanced standards of the rest of the station, Jerry thought, watching DeShawn adjust something in Arti's head. Obviously, once again nobody had ever expected anything to go wrong so they'd never thought about actually having to use it.

He felt stiff with tension as he peered at the tiny image on the little screen. Since she was wearing the communications package on her chest, he couldn't see Ailee herself and that worried him. They hadn't got sound, either. DeShawn was still adjusting wires in Arti's head to get radio contact with Ailee, but no success yet.

"What're those?" Jerry asked, pointing, as U-shaped pieces of metal loomed into view.

"Handholds," DeShawn said. "Places to secure the tether so a kid who's checking the skin for damage from comet debris can work without having it get in the way, or without the danger of drifting off."

"Why not just send a 'bot?"

"There are some things humans do better than 'bots," DeShawn replied.

Jerry watched the screen for a while without talking.

"I have the antenna in view," Ailee's voice said suddenly through Jerry's earplug. Her voice sounded small and tinny and very far away.

Now the monitor showed a view up the slope of the science module. The lamp in Ailee's helmet illuminated an array of dish antennae and looming radio spires on one of the projecting booms heading off at right angles from the four modules. Where the helmet's light didn't touch Oort One, the background of space looked very black.

"Can you reach it safely?" DeShawn asked.

"Affirmative," Ailee said. "Heading there now."

"Roger," DeShawn said.

"Secure tether now," Arti instructed.

"Tether secure, check," Ailee said.

Jerry concentrated on the bobbing image on the monitor. Now he could see one of Ailee's gloved hands on the boom, the other reaching out to the frozen antenna. They were bulky gloves, he thought; it must be hard to do anything delicate wearing them. He realized he was holding his breath again and let it go.

"Making contact with the antenna now," Ailee said.

"Switching monitor image to antenna," Arti said.

DeShawn bent over Arti's head. The tiny screen blurred. Gray mist swirled.

"Checking," Arti said. "Realign antenna to following coordinates."

Jerry was too nervous to pay much attention to the strings of data exchanged between Ailee and the AI after that. Adrenaline flowing through his blood made his heart beat faster and his breathing come shallower. Fight or flight, he thought; humans still had the same reactions to danger as that smilodon Nan had gone to fetch. He would've felt better if he could've done something to help, but all he could do now was wait.

For the first time he understood how Nan felt when she objected to long discussions of things. He liked to think things over and she liked to act; maybe they made good coleaders after all. Easier to decide that when she wasn't around to annoy him, he thought with a brief smile.

"No joy," Arti said.

"Trying again," Ailee said.

"Roger," the AI replied.

It was almost amusing how the old space jargon had survived. Jerry thought. But why shouldn't it have? Space activities demanded a different language, simpler, clearer than ordinary verbal exchanges. His father would have said there was no room for misunderstanding in space.

"Switching back to your suitcam," Arti said.

The on-screen mist cleared, giving the view of the antenna he'd been watching a moment ago. It was almost like watching one of the NASA spacewalks that Jerry had seen a dozen times at the Imax theater. But even those giant screens couldn't make it as exciting and nerve-wracking as the real thing.

"Ah. I think I've figured out the problem," Arti said. "Sending new coordinates."

"I copy," Ailee said.

Something ropy snaked across the screen and Jerry

recognized a section of the umbilical tether that had floated in front of the vidcam's lens.

Ailee gasped. "Arti! My tether is unsecured!"

Jerry's heart thudded. "How could that've happened?"

"Stay calm, Ailee," DeShawn said. "Grab the nearest handhold. You'll be all right."

"Got it." Ailee's voice sounded shaky. "I must not have connected it properly somehow. It's been a long time since I practiced this."

And those gloves are way too clumsy, Jerry thought.

"Mission accomplished," Arti said. "The antenna's working. And just in time! I am picking up the arrival of a shuttle from Edge Two, ETA in ten minutes, twenty-two seconds. Come back in now, Ailee. Carefully."

"Take it slowly," DeShawn warned. "Don't let go of one handhold until you have the next one in your grasp."

"Roger," Ailee said. "But they're awfully far apart."

DeShawn said, "You did it on the way up, Ailee. You can do it again."

Jerry stared intently at the monitor showing hands in the bulky space gloves crawling at a snail's pace across the skin of the science module, moving cautiously from one handhold to the next toward the open doors of Airlock B and safety. He could see what a stretch it was for her; the handholds seemed to have been positioned with somebody bigger in mind.

"Not much farther, Ailee," DeShawn encouraged. "You're almost there."

Then Ailee screamed.

"What happened?" Jerry yelled.

"One hand slipped off," Arti said. "Before the other had caught the next handhold."

"She's totally loose in space?" Jerry heard his voice come out high-pitched with fear. "What're we going to do?"

Arti ignored him. "Ailee? Grab onto whatever you can and hold on."

The screen showed a jumble of images as if the camera were doing flipflops.

It seemed like a terribly long time before Ailee's voice said shakily through the earphones, "I slipped a long way, Arti. A really long way. I bumped into another antenna on the boom. I'm holding it now."

"Good girl," Arti said.

"Now what?" Jerry demanded.

The AI said, "Somebody will need to go outside and get her."

30

Nan and Will emerged from the t-port and crossed the hall at Edge Two, heading for the shuttle dock as fast as they could. Smiley seemed irritable and kept pulling at the leash. Maybe his legs felt rubbery on the trip, Nan thought, just as hers had that first time. She made soothing, clucking noises at the cub.

The news that they were coming, accompanied by a smilodon, had obviously reached Edge Two. Curious faces stared at them from behind half-closed doors, looking as if the kids who owned the faces were ready to slam the doors quickly if necessary. But Doctor Arlo Pike was nowhere in sight. Nan led Smiley into the lock where the cub sat down as if he were tired.

"This beast scarce fits a seatweb," Will said suddenly. "How then shall we keep him peaceful on a voyage of more than two hours to Oort One?"

Will was right; that could be a problem. Then a tall boy with black spiky hair came into the lock; he was wearing a black jumpsuit covered with ribbons and tassels in a rainbow of colors that made her think of dancers or rock musicians. He carried what looked like a plastic picnic cooler.

"We thought you might need a little help," he said,

handing the cooler to Nan. "So we had our synthesizer make up a very large bone."

She lifted the lid and peeked inside. It looked big enough to be the thigh bone of a moose, and there was just enough meat on it to keep Smiley busy, but not enough to dull his appetite so he wouldn't want to go hunting Thogs. Catching a whiff of something good to chew on, Smiley lifted his head and sniffed the air.

"I hope it's the right kind for a smilodon," the guy said. "We don't know much about meat."

She said, "It'll be an appetizer for him."

"We've also loaded some more food supplies for the station," the guy said. "Good luck!"

"Thanks," she said.

Will grabbed up the cooler and together the two of them and the smilodon cub entered the shuttle.

The bone was almost gone by the time the shuttle slid up against Airlock A, and Smiley was yawning sleepily. But he came wide awake as the doors opened and he got his first sight of Oort One. They entered Command.

"Where be our friends?" Will asked, glancing around. He called, "Ailee? Jerry?"

Nobody answered. In the silence, a lone Thog rolled slowly down the center of the module.

Nan had her hand on Smiley's harness, and she felt the fur on his hackles rising. "Easy, boy," she said.

"Let him go," Will whispered.

She released her hold. There was a blur of motion as Smiley sprang forward. Unprepared for the lower gravity, the cub hit his target midleap and kept on going until he and the Thog in his mouth hit the opposite wall, where the cub lay for a second, splay-legged, looking surprised. Then Smiley licked his lips.

"He swallowed it whole!" she said.

"Well done!" Will clapped his hands.

"Almost makes you feel sorry for the Thogs, doesn't it?" she said with a grin.

The cub stood up again, his massive head moving slowly from side to side, searching for dinner. His dagger teeth gleamed in the station's bright lights.

Nan glanced round too. At least the lights were working. But the last time she'd been up here, there'd been Thogs all over the place; now the module seemed clean. Too clean. She felt disappointed. Maybe the cats Ailee had brought up had learned to be better hunters? Not likely, she thought, remembering their poor record. How big would a ball of Thogs have to be before Smiley couldn't swallow it? Pretty big indeed.

"Let's do this systematically," she said. "We'll try to clear one module at a time, starting with Habitat because it was the worst infested."

She grabbed Smiley's harness again and the three of them set off through the airtight doors of the transfer node and down the connecting corridor to Habitat.

In Habitat, they came upon a chaotic scene. Thogs were everywhere, on the chairs and the table in the galley, on the shelves and the useless food synthesizer.

"Looks like the 'Tribbles' episode from *Star Trek*!" she said.

Smiley charged into the middle of the first group of Thogs he saw and began gulping them down, not even taking the time to chew. The rest of the alien fur balls scattered at his approach and rolled swiftly away.

"O wondrous sight!" Will said. "How my captain would have loved thee, fierce beast!"

Nan moved on. Entering the cubicle she'd shared with Ailee, she saw a small cluster of cats on one of the bunks.

"Where be the others?" Will asked. He stood in the doorway just behind her, looking over her shoulder.

She counted the cats. Five. The Siamese female, two calico females, one black-and-white male, and one tabby male. Had there been other casualties?

Smiley padded into the cubicle and yawned, revealing his impressive array of teeth. For a moment, she was afraid he'd consider the little half-grown cats as another course in this wonderful meal he was having.

But as if his yawn was some kind of signal, the Siamese and one of the calicos stood up, arched their backs, swelled the fur out on their tails and hissed.

Surprised, the saber-toothed tiger cub sat back on his haunches and leaned against Nan's leg. He was so heavy, she had to grab the edge of a bunk for support. He made a little noise that sounded to her suspiciously like "meow."

She laughed. "Maybe Jerry was right after all. You're a *cat*, Smiley. And these ladies just reminded you of your manners!"

Then a Thog rolled off one of the bunks and streaked for the door. In the blink of an eye, Smiley was after it, bounding clumsily in the low gravity. Nan and Will followed him out the door just in time to see three more Thogs slide into view down the hallway. All four Thogs met a second before Smiley reached them, jaws stretched wide to engulf the target.

Her breath caught in her throat. She saw the blur

of gray fur as the Thogs seemed to fly together like iron filings jumping to a magnet.

She blinked. The Thogs had disappeared and Smiley was once again licking his lips.

"Yay!" she yelled. "Smiley, you did it!"

The three searched the module together. No more Thogs appeared. The aliens seemed to sense Smiley was a bigger danger than the cats and were hiding. Better in the walls than out in the open, forming balls and damaging the station, she remembered.

This was going to be so easy now that Smiley was on the team. The cub would swallow the Thogs up like a monster vacuum cleaner sucking up hairballs. And if that didn't completely take care of the problem, then at least he'd scare them into staying out of sight in the walls where they were less dangerous.

There was nothing the aliens could do against this secret weapon from Earth's prehistoric past. Thogs were pathetic. *Game's over,* Nan thought. *We've saved the station!*

The cub began to lick one of his paws. Soon he was rubbing the wet paw over the fur behind his ears, washing himself like an overgrown household cat. She plopped down on the floor beside him and put her arms around his neck. Smiley stopped washing for a second and ran his rough tongue over her cheek. As he did so, one of the long dagger teeth brushed lightly over her skin.

Will shivered. "You be braver than I, Nan."

"Smiley wouldn't hurt me," she said. "We're friends."

"For the nonce," Will said soberly.

She stood up again. "You're probably right. Let's

get back to work till he's full. Or exhausted. Then when we find the others, we can tell them the good news. The problem's already solved."

"But where be they?" Will said.

31

"There's no other solution," Arti said. "Someone will need to go outside and bring Ailee in."

"We don't have another spacesuit," DeShawn pointed out.

"What!" Jerry said. "How can that happen?"

DeShawn looked embarrassed. "We had two, but Gar was wearing the other one when we had the accident I told you about."

Jerry shook his head. "Can't we use the shuttle?"

"Fortunately, the shuttle has just docked," Arti announced. "Nan and Will have just disembarked with the smilodon cub."

"So send the shuttle to Ailee immediately!" Jerry said. The smilodon would have to wait.

"I'm afraid I can't do that, Jerry," Arti replied. He hung his head like Rufus did when he knew he was in trouble. "You see, the shuttle's set up to make the regular run between the station and Edge Two without a pilot, but anything else would take a lot of reprogramming."

"The main computers must have all that stuff in them," he began angrily. Then he remembered; the Thogs had damaged the station's computers and they still weren't working. He took a deep breath. "All right. Then one of us will have to pilot the shuttle manually.''

"It's difficult to maneuver a shuttle this close to the station,'' DeShawn pointed out.

"What other choice do we have?'' Jerry said grimly. As team leader, he had to take command.

He raced through the connector from the SRL back to Airlock A with bounding leaps, pushing himself off the walls on either side as he bumped into them. He was glad—finally!—to have something he could do in this emergency.

The great feeling of relief from taking action helped him push down the little voice deep inside that kept telling him *This is going to be dangerous, you don't know what you're about to do, you aren't strong enough.* The voice sounded just like his mother. He ignored it.

He reached the doors and punched the control panel where a blue light showed the presence of the shuttle and a green light turned red as the doors slid open.

As he stepped inside, DeShawn caught up with him.

"Jerry! Wait!'' DeShawn said. "What do you know about flying a shuttle?''

"Piece of cake!'' he said, giving DeShawn a thumbs up. "Just like driving a car.''

"Do you *know* how to drive a car?'' DeShawn challenged.

"I've taken driver's ed,'' he said with a grin. "How difficult can it be?''

He touched the panel inside the airlock and the doors slid closed. The outer doors opened into the shuttle.

Famous last words, he thought gloomily, staring at the control panel of the little shuttle. But he hadn't been about to let DeShawn know how nervous he really was. He fastened the seatweb in the pilot's chair. Although onboard AIs usually flew the shuttle between Edge Two and the station, it was set up to be manually operated if needed.

Now he faced a daunting display of gauges and switches and square buttons waiting for him to press. It was a bit like the diagrams in *The Space Shuttle Operator's Manual* that a friend brought him back from Space Camp one time. He remembered poring over the drawings and the procedures, wondering how he was ever going to get his mother to let him go.

Main engine status, he read now. *Tank. Abort mode. Event sequence. Pitch. Roll. Yaw. Docking. Radar. Power—*

Power. He pressed that one and a soft tremor ran through the shuttle. A speed scale lit. He selected the lowest speed it offered. Best to start slow while he was learning how to do it. Now what?

Release. That seemed obvious. He touched it and sensed the shuttle gently freeing itself from Oort One's grip like a butterfly lifting off his hand. The craft moved smoothly away from the airlock. There ought to be a control stick to steer with, he thought. Then he saw it. It looked something like the shift lever in a car.

His heart pounded. He pulled back slowly on the stick. Back raised the craft's nose, down lowered it. Left and right were obvious. He guided the shuttle slowly, trying to keep it level but wobbling a bit at first, flying low over the connector and the science module toward the extended boom where the rows of antennae and radar dishes were located.

Unlike the space station, the shuttle had a forward window. Below him, Oort One turned slowly, its silver skin gleaming softly in the circle of the little craft's searchlight. Ahead, he saw the vast blackness of deep space sprinkled with the steady white beacons of the stars.

For a second, he felt so awed by the majestic scene that he sat and stared, forgetting to steer. Then, as he guided the shuttle to follow the curve of the module below him, the view swung away from the galaxy. Now he was looking back inward, across the solar system, until he could see the bright point of the sun itself. So tiny, he thought, and so very far away. Somewhere back there, too small and dim to see from this vast distance, was Planet Earth itself. Home.

Then the searchlight picked out Ailee in her silver spacesuit clinging to one of the bowl-shaped structures ahead of him on the boom. He had to be extremely careful at this point. If he approached too fast, he risked bumping the antenna and damaging the shuttle. He could even knock Ailee off into space. He shivered at the thought.

He frowned at the control panel again. The speed gauge appeared to be at its lowest register, but even that seemed a bit fast to rendezvous with Ailee. Maybe he should just shut off the power? That wasn't exactly right either, but if he selected it, maybe inertia would keep him moving forward slowly. On Earth, everything has friction and that's what slows it down. Without the gravity of a planet to affect the shuttle, physics said the craft should drift on forever. Or at least, he thought hastily, until he started up the engines again.

He depressed the power button. That seemed to work. The shuttle was now drifting along the length of the slowly rotating boom. The forward window was almost level with Ailee now. She let go of the antenna with one hand and waved at him.

And as Jerry stared back at her, he realized the shuttle was going to drift right on by and leave her behind.

Do something, fool! he told himself. But what? How was he going to brake this thing?

Panicked, he searched the control panel. "Brakes" wasn't a word he expected to find there. But he did see a small lever next to the pilot's seat marked *Reverse Thrusters.*

He pushed the lever as far as it would go, and the shuttle gave an answering shudder and slowed even more. But it still glided past Ailee clinging to the antenna. Then as he began to despair of getting it right, the shuttle came to a stop, then slowly started to inch backward.

Now his fingers gripped the lever tightly. He had to get this just right; it wouldn't do to go whizzing past Ailee again, this time in reverse! He could feel the shuttle trembling as he sent conflicting commands to reverse and to go forward. This wasn't the right way to stop it, but it would have to do.

He managed to bring the craft level with Ailee. Glancing out the forward window, he could just make out her expression through the faceplate in her helmet as she grabbed hold of the shuttle. She was smiling at her rescuer.

Jerry felt like a complete idiot to have come all this way only to have no plan for what to do next. How was he going to get Ailee inside the shuttle?

He couldn't just open the door and let her step in. Vacuum would suck him out immediately. She had a space suit on and didn't need to come inside, but if she clung to the outside while he took the shuttle back then there'd be the problem of getting her inside the airlock when they docked. He couldn't see a solution.

She was pointing at something at the back of the shuttle. Something she wanted him to see.

"What is it?" he said, looking over his shoulder.

She moved her hand and pointed inside through the forward window. He frowned. He had no idea what she meant. If only he knew how to patch in to her communications with Arti, maybe they'd come up with something. He stared at the control panel.

Environment control. Exterior temperature. Air data probe.

Nothing there that would help get Ailee inside.

And then he saw it. *Cargo bay*, the button said. He depressed it and Ailee waved immediately.

Of course. The shuttle had a small bay that opened to space for ferrying construction materials to the station. He couldn't see the cargo bay's doors from the pilot's seat, but Ailee headed back along the shuttle's spine and disappeared from his view. He felt the little craft rock slightly as she entered.

"I'm on board, Jerry," Ailee's voice said suddenly over the shuttle's intercom. "Close the cargo bay doors now."

Relief flooded over him. She was safe. He'd done it. He'd had to make it up the whole way, but he'd done it. This must be what old-time pilots called "flying by the seat of your pants," he decided. He was so excited he wanted to yell.

Instead, he asked in a low voice, "Are you all right?"

"Yes," Ailee said. "Thanks to you, Jerry. I'm so grateful to you! That was a wonderful thing you just did. The history books are right in what they said about you—'' She stopped abruptly as if she'd said too much. Then she added, "You really are a hero!"

He felt his cheeks turning fiery red under her praise. It was good that she couldn't see him right now.

"Piece of cake!" he said.

32

The next morning, Smiley bounded down the connector toward the SRL after several rolling blurs. There must've been at least six Thogs, Nan thought. But they'd be no match for their eighty-pound pursuer, who was all muscle and heart.

The rest of the team, Will included, were in the control center this morning. Jerry had seemed calmer somehow, less ready to show off his knowledge, and Nan found that a relief.

Smiley didn't seem to notice the mental effect the Thogs used on humans. The cats didn't either. It couldn't be just a matter of intelligence; Smiley wasn't dumb. Perhaps it had to do with sentience, being self-aware. What was that saying one of her teachers back in Santa Marta had told them? *I think, therefore I am.* Smiley obviously didn't think much about his existence, and that might be exactly what gave him immunity to the Thogs.

Or perhaps it explained why the Thogs weren't interested in the cats or Smiley. That was an odd idea she might think about when she had time.

The Thogs, with Smiley in hot pursuit, rolled through the transfer node into the SRL. She came through just in time to see the Thogs backed against the far end with no escape left.

In a flash, they had formed into a ball that she estimated must've been about ten inches in diameter. Smiley skidded toward them. The smilodon's huge jaw seemed to come unhinged. The lower half sank until the opening was enormous, the long daggers poised to strike. The sign at the zoo had said that jaw could open 120 degrees. Nan believed it now. It looked like an animal version of a bulldozer's earth-moving shovel with jagged iron teeth.

Then the jaws snapped shut and the Thogs disappeared.

Smiley burped.

Happy as she was to see it happen, she couldn't help shivering. "I'm sure glad you're my friend, not my enemy, Smiley."

She added these Thogs to the count she was making on her e-pad. The cub had already finished off twenty balls this morning since they'd been up, with anywhere from two to six aliens in each ball. Quite a breakfast. She must be sure to remember that it wasn't nutritious and give him the supplements.

Some of the balls had been pretty big. Sooner or later, one ball was bound to be too big for Smiley to swallow. Then what? *Cross that bridge when you get to it,* she told herself.

"Come on, Smiley," she said, catching the cub by the harness. "We need to check all the cubicles for strays."

Smiley responded by butting his head against Nan's arm the way a cat does when it wants to be petted. He stood just higher than her waist now; when he was finished growing, he was going to be huge. She scratched the cub's head, and again she heard that rumble of a purr in his throat. It was hard not to like him, she thought, he was such an affectionate baby.

They went to work. She pushed open the first door and found it led to a large laboratory cubicle where somebody had been doing biology experiments before the food emergency had sent Oort One's crew home. On a long bench against one curving wall, she saw rows of tall jars and glass boxes full of bees and spiders. It looked like it might have been a fun project, except for the spiders.

Smiley trotted inside obediently and sniffed around. Two lone Thogs fled for the safety of the walls as soon as the smilodon appeared, leaving the cubicle empty.

They tried the second, where Jerry had done the dissection, then opened a third door with similar results. The Thogs didn't come out of the walls once they noticed Smiley.

Something Will said a long time ago was still bothering Nan. The enemy always wants something from you: your life, your ship, or your treasure. So what did the Thogs want? Individually they might not have brains, but they managed to get to Oort One and disrupt the space station, didn't they? Any race that powerful would be a terrific force in the galaxy, she thought. Think what they could achieve—

If they had hands.

Was that it? They couldn't build. Maybe they would need to take over and control a race that had hands to build the things they wanted. She didn't have enough science to know if this were possible or not.

"Nothing here, Smiley," she said, glancing into the fourth cubicle in a row without seeing Thogs.

Somebody had been doing hydroponics experi-

ments in here before they'd been sent home. She saw
the young plants growing in their nutrient-rich con-
tainers; some of them looked a bit bedraggled, showing the absence of their caretakers already. Why
would the Oort One crew have worried about growing plants when the synthesizer could make just
about everything, she wondered? Library would
know.

That reminded her of something else that was bothering her. She moved quickly across the cubicle to a
computer terminal and called up Library.

"Good morning, Nan," Library said. "What help
do you need today?"

"Doctor Cee told us these aliens were called 'Thogemags,' " she said. "Where did she get the name
from? Has anybody other than us met the Thogs?"

"To answer your second question first," Library
said. "If any other alien species have made contact
with the Thogemags, we don't know about them."

"But they came with a dumb name."

"It was meant as a kind of joke, since we suspected
they were a hive-mind species," Library said. "It
stands for 'a THOusand GErbils MAke a Genius.' "

"Like the idea that if you put a thousand monkeys
in a room with a thousand typewriters?" she guessed.
"After a while they'll come up with Shakespeare's
plays."

"Something like that," Library agreed. "Is there
any other information I can help you with?"

She shook her head. "Not right now."

The monkey idea had always sounded stupid.
Maybe the explanation about the Thogs was equally
off-base. She decided to go over to the command
module where the others were. There was an idea at
the back of her mind that she couldn't quite seem to

get out in the open where she could think about it. Talking things over with Jerry would help.

Wow! she thought. That had to be a first, asking Jerry for his opinion on anything! But it felt nice to have someone to share problems with for a change.

Smiley dawdled behind her in the cubicle as if he wasn't convinced there were no more Thogs to be rooted out.

Just as she headed to the transfer node, a door to a small cubicle they hadn't searched opened, and a man stepped out, carrying a glass pot with a dead plant in one hand.

It was Doctor Arlo Pike.

Nan's heart did a somersault in her chest.

"Doctor Pike?" she stammered, staring up at the tall man with a thin face and an expression that looked as if he'd just tasted something bitter. "What're you doing on Oort One?"

"I could ask the same about you, young lady!" the man said.

"But how did you get here?"

"I came over by shuttle from Edge Two, like everybody else," he said. "How do you imagine I did it?"

She frowned. There was something not quite right here. It was definitely Pike, the bad-tempered scientist, but he seemed a bit off somehow, like a photo that was out of focus. She could recognize who it was, but the details seemed fuzzy. For instance, she didn't remember Pike's hair being quite so long. And had Pike always had that little scar above his left eye?

"You're Nan Smith, aren't you?" Pike demanded.

"Well, of course I am," she said, bewildered.

"Right!" Pike said, sounding satisfied. "And now

I intend to take you into custody until you can be returned to Earth and sent packing.''

"What for?''

"For jeopardizing crucial experiments,'' he said, waving the dead plant in her face. "Evidence! Don't you realize this research is for the benefit of future space colonies? We need to find ways to produce food quickly and cheaply in places where there are no synthesizers. You've destroyed years of valuable work!''

"I did nothing of the sort!'' she protested.

Pike dropped the plant—the glass bounced but didn't break—and grabbed her arm with his left hand.

"Hey!'' she yelled.

Doctor Pike strode quickly toward the transfer node, dragging her along with him. "Hurry up!''

"What're you doing?'' she demanded, struggling. "Let me go!''

He'd caught her off-guard, before she could block him. That was a mistake she shouldn't have made. "Action in tranquillity,'' Grampa Hong used to teach her. She'd lost her center of peace so she couldn't act when she needed to. A bad mistake. She might not get another chance.

Reaching the transfer node, Pike jerked Nan's arm hard so she stumbled cross the threshold before the node's door had fully opened. He kept on going toward the node's opposite door.

"Smiley!'' she yelled.

The cub emerged from the cubicle. In front of him there was a huge ball of Thogs, rolling furiously away. All the lights in the SRL flickered and went out, including all the monitor lights on the computer terminals. But she could still hear Smiley bounding toward her.

Just as the cub came through the first door to the transfer node, Pike was dragging Nan through the second door. Then he slammed a hand against a panel on the curving wall. The door closed, leaving Smiley trapped in the transfer node.

33

The lights in the command module flickered.

"Not again!" Jerry moaned.

He waited, but luckily nothing else seemed to be happening. The four of them were working in Command with Arti, getting the new communications unit to bypass the station's damaged computers. At least, three of them had been working: Jerry, DeShawn, and Ailee. Will was an interested spectator.

DeShawn gently brushed off a little cat that jumped onto the computer's keyboard. He called up the three-dimensional display of Oort One. Four blue "people" dots flashed at them from Command where they were. DeShawn keyed in another set of instructions. The blinking stars vanished, and data flowed over the screen.

"The transfer node into the SRL seems to have locked," DeShawn said, sounding surprised. "We don't lock the nodes unless they've been damaged. It must've malfunctioned."

Ailee leaned over DeShawn's shoulder to stare at the screen.

"Thogs, of course," Jerry suggested.

DeShawn ran one finger over the display.

"I don't see any of them anywhere out in the open

on the station right now," DeShawn said, studying the screen. "That means the smilodon's chased them back into the walls."

"If not Thogs, then some devil hath caused the light to comport itself like a fizgig," Will pointed out as the lights flickered overhead again.

"A what?" Ailee asked. "My language nannie missed that one."

Will turned pink and wouldn't explain. Whatever the word meant, Jerry thought, it obviously wasn't fit for polite company.

He stared down at the AI. "We're doing much better with Smiley here. But I guess he can't take care of all of them all of the time."

"As long as he manages to keep large numbers of them from crowding together," Ailee said, "then we're better off than before."

"Doctor Pike has a theory about a possible crisis point," Arti explained. "A critical number of the aliens creating some huge, probably dangerous effect."

"I don't remember him using that term," Jerry said.

"Yes," DeShawn agreed. "He discussed it with me the last time he was here. That's one of the reasons we try not to scare them into large groupings."

"You know Pike?" Jerry asked. "And he was *here*?"

DeShawn looked puzzled. "Well, sure."

"Ah," Arti said. "I think there's a slight misunderstanding here, a need for clarification. You see—"

"Where's Nan?" Ailee interrupted suddenly. "I haven't seen her for hours."

Will answered. "She hath taken the beast on the hunt."

"Could she have been accidentally locked in when the transfer node malfunctioned?" Jerry asked.

DeShawn ran his fingers over the keyboard again, then stared at the screen. "No. Nobody's in the SRL."

"I be not at ease with this!" Will said.

Jerry patted the worried boy on the shoulder. "Let's try looking elsewhere, DeShawn."

DeShawn nodded his agreement. "Maybe she went down to the LUM," he suggested.

DeShawn called up each module's diagram in turn. But the Logistics and Utilities Module also showed empty on the screen. So did Habitat. And they knew she wasn't in Command with them. Nan Smith seemed to have disappeared off the space station.

"Perchance the thing doth not work right," Will said, pointing to the computer terminal.

Jerry looked at DeShawn. "At the least, we could unlock that stuck transfer node," he suggested.

"Okay," DeShawn agreed. "Arti, I've got you fully patched in. You stay and monitor the computers."

They crowded through the transfer node and hurried down the connecting corridor to the SRL, Will in the lead. At the malfunctioning transfer node, DeShawn knelt down and raised a small metal panel in the floor. Jerry bent over to watch; DeShawn adjusted something he couldn't see.

When they finally got the door open, an anxious Smiley came tumbling out, almost knocking Jerry over in his haste. The animal was bigger and bulkier than his own dog. Rufus stood almost two feet tall, not counting his head, but this cub was at least six inches taller than the Irish setter, and much heavier. Judging from the scratch marks made by the smilodon's claws on the walls, Jerry understood the cub hadn't enjoyed being caged up in the locked node.

"The smilodon looks hungry," DeShawn said. "When's Nan going to feed him?"

"Soon," Will replied. "He hunts better on an empty belly."

Jerry said, "I wouldn't want to cross him when he thinks he's starving!"

Ailee came out of the SRL. "Nobody's in here."

"Perchance Nan hath gone back to Habitat?" Will said. He looked hopeful. "Perchance she prepares lunch."

Jerry wasn't willing to admit it, but he had started to have a bad feeling about Nan's disappearance. So apparently had Ailee and DeShawn. They crowded and bumped each other in their haste to get back through the transfer node and down the corridor to Habitat. Will was first once again. Smiley loped along with them.

Half an hour later, after searching every cubicle, looking under every bunk, opening every cupboard and hatch in the dorms and the galley, they hadn't found so much as one small Thog. And they had to admit Nan wasn't in Habitat.

"I can't think of any place else to look," DeShawn said.

They were all disheartened. Even Will agreed it was useless to search any longer. The Elizabethan kid looked fierce, Jerry thought, but this time he wasn't the first one into the transfer node, he was last. They all turned slowly back through the node and headed down the corridor.

Then Will whispered, "Smiley knows where Nan be. Look at him!"

Jerry whirled round, almost losing his balance because he'd forgotten about fast movements in low gravity. The smilodon cub stood behind them, staring down the corridor, head low. The hackles of his neck stood straight up as if he'd just caught sight of an enemy. His top lip lifted in a bad-tempered snarl that made the dagger teeth seem enormous.

Will took a step toward the smilodon.

Horrified, Jerry grabbed Will and pulled him back.

"Unhand me!" Will said angrily, shaking Jerry's fingers off his sleeve. "We cannot find Nan, but this cat surely will!"

"He's dangerous," Jerry warned.

Somehow, when Nan had suggested this next move, he'd overlooked the fact that they'd be playing with an animal that wasn't just extinct, it was also ferocious. There was no way not to notice that fact now. He was starting to have a very bad feeling about this. Bringing the cub up wasn't the team's best idea. The sooner Smiley went back to the zoo the better.

"He's not a pet, Will," DeShawn said. "He's a wild animal. He could kill you."

"But the beast loves Nan!" Will argued.

"He's right," Ailee put in. "If Nan is around here somewhere, maybe hurt, Smiley could sniff her out."

Will suddenly darted forward and grabbed Smiley by the harness. "I have no treat to give thee, Beauty, like thy own Lady Nan doth give. But I have need of thy services!"

Smiley bounded clumsily down the corridor dragging Will with him.

"We've already searched the LUM," Jerry said. "Why's he heading back there?"

"He's heading for Command!" Ailee said. "But Nan couldn't be in there. That's where we were."

"No, he's heading for the airlock," DeShawn added.

"If she was in the airlock, it would've showed up in the diagram, wouldn't it?" Jerry asked.

"I made the search request module by module," DeShawn said. "I could've requested a search for human presence instead, but I thought the other was preferable. I apologize if I made an error in judgement."

"Oh, don't be so stuffy!" Jerry said. "We've all made mistakes here."

They skidded to a halt by the outer door of Airlock A.

Jerry stared at the control panel. "Someone's boarding the shuttle!" he said.

34

"**Y**ou can't make me go!" Nan protested.

Doctor Pike held her firmly by the arm and pushed her into Airlock A. She wriggled and pulled against him. But she couldn't get loose.

That was another thing wrong. Arlo Pike had been so easy to throw when she'd arrived through the time tunnel. No way he could've learned kung fu or karate so fast!

Pike's right hand grasped her arm tightly while his left hand feverishly tried to key the right sequence into the airlock's control pad to close the doors. Same face, same nasty temper, Nan thought. But this guy was apparently left-handed. Whoever he was, he was definitely not Arlo Pike.

He was worse. She bucked and twisted in his grasp; if she couldn't free her arm, at least she'd make sure it was very difficult for him to reach the pad.

"You can't defeat me," the man boasted. "I work out all the time on Edge Two. I have three black belts!"

"You're not Arlo Pike," she said, figuring it out. "But you could be his twin brother."

The man glanced at her. "Of course I am! I thought you knew that? My name's Milo Pike. Arlo and I are in frequent radio contact. He told me you'd thrust yourself into this team where you didn't belong, jeopardizing the mission. I came over to check on you. And I found you destroying the hydroponics experiment.''

''That's not true!'' she protested.

On the pad, a light glowed. The airlock doors sighed shut.

''Now.'' Milo Pike grinned at her. ''I'll open the shuttle and we'll go aboard.''

For one second as he turned back to the control pad, his attention wavered. His right hand loosened its grip. Nan was centered and ready this time. She wrenched her arm free and at the same time kicked him hard in the leg, right on the shinbone where it would hurt most.

Milo Pike gasped and hugged his leg with both hands. She lunged for the controls to reopen the door. Pike let go of his leg and grabbed her around the waist. She flailed at him with her fists, kicked backward with her heels, used her nails on his hands. Grampa Hong might not have approved of her form, but this wasn't a friendly competition.

Muffled shouts came from the other side of the airlock's inner door. She was too busy to pay attention.

Pike got the outer door open, revealing the shuttle.

''In we go!'' he said, giving her a shove.

Nan made a huge last effort and slammed her fist down on the control pad as he dragged her past. The doors leading to the shuttle closed again.

Pike screeched and tried to get to the pad. She struggled harder to pull him off balance.

The inner door slid open. A huge golden brown shape appeared. A deep growl filled the airlock.

''Smiley!'' she yelled.

The cub saw her and sprang. But Pike was between him and Nan. She caught a flash of long smilodon teeth.

Milo Pike went down under the smilodon—who stood on him like a big friendly cat.

Then Will was there too, helping her pull Smiley off. Pike seemed too scared to move even when Smiley's weight was removed from his chest. He lay curled up in a ball, arms over his head.

Smiley pushed his nose hard against Nan's hip. She responded by hugging him. His big tongue lapped her arm. For a moment, she tussled with him as if he were an overgrown kitten, ducking his claws and teeth.

"Nan! Are you okay?"

Jerry's voice distracted her, pulling her attention away. In that second, a claw caught her forearm, leaving a long red gash. She looked down at the cut; blood oozed out.

"Here. Let me look." DeShawn pushed past Jerry and knelt beside Nan.

"He didn't do it on purpose," she said quickly.

"It's not deep, luckily," DeShawn said. "There's a first-aid kit just down the hall—"

Ailee ran to get it.

"Who's this?" Jerry said. He'd just noticed the man curled up on the floor. "Doctor Pike? But it can't be!"

"Doctor Milo Pike," Arti said. The computer-dog stood just outside the airlock. "I believe you've met his twin brother."

DeShawn said to Milo Pike, "You can get up now and explain yourself."

Pike moaned and peered through his fingers at them. Will aimed a kick in his direction, but DeShawn stopped him.

"Whatever he's been doing," DeShawn said, "we'll take him to Edge Two to face the authorities. That's our way."

Ailee returned with the antiseptic salve and applied it to Nan's arm. "It might leave a bit of a scar, Nan. But it'll heal fast and won't get infected."

"No cat scratch fever, you mean?" She gave Ailee a wobbly grin.

"Right." Ailee smiled back.

"Thanks." Nan put an arm around Smiley, who was panting anxiously; his breath felt hot against her cheek. She could feel the tiny vibration of a growl in his throat. He shoved his head against her hip again.

"It's okay, Smiley boy," she said. "Don't be nervous."

Milo Pike stood up and glared round at them. "I've dedicated my life to my work on Edge Two," he said. "Then *children* allowed this problem with the Thogs to happen! Careless children who let aliens stow away in their luggage. There are no problems up here that adults couldn't solve if we could get at them."

"Well, that's a problem in itself," Jerry said reasonably. "You can't."

Milo Pike scowled at him. "My brother says we have to use whatever weapons we can in this fight. I can respect what history says about you, Jerry. But we don't have to put up with trash like her." He pointed at Nan. "A juvenile delinquent! A street kid who thinks being on a space station is just a game! A—"

"Your words be fit for the jakes, not for the company of good people!" Will said angrily.

Smiley gave a low warning growl.

Milo Pike turned and took two quick steps back toward the shuttle.

Smiley bounded right out of Nan's arms and knocked him down again. There was nothing friendly about it this time; his instinct to hunt prey had been triggered. Pike screamed. It took all the strength of Jerry, DeShawn, Will, and Nan combined to drag Smiley off. Pike held up one arm and went on bellowing loudly, a sound that told Nan he was more terrified than hurt.

Then Smiley pulled his head out of Nan's arms and snarled, and the team backed off hurriedly. His long dagger teeth slashed through the air, narrowly missing them.

"It's okay, Smiley," Nan coaxed. "You can relax now." But she was shaking with fright. This was a different Smiley all of a sudden, nervous, unpredictable.

"Nan!" Ailee said urgently. "The tranquilizer they gave you? Smiley needs it now!"

Will added quietly, "The beast hath tasted man's blood, Nan. Observe him."

Smiley crouched by the airlock's outer doors. The saber teeth were red-tipped with Milo Pike's blood. As she watched, the pink tongue flicked out and licked the teeth clean. His golden cat's eyes closed lazily, then blinked open again, watching Nan.

She felt her skin prickling with fear.

Shakily, Nan took a step toward Smiley, holding her left hand to him in a fist, palm down. But she still couldn't believe he'd hurt her. In her pocket, her right hand closed over the small jet spray syringe that contained the animal tranquilizer.

The smilodon sniffed at her left hand as if he'd forgotten who she was. Could he smell her fear? He seemed enormous all of a sudden. She fought down a wave of panic.

The smilodon allowed her to come up close, but he sniffed the back of her hand suspiciously again. She took her other hand slowly out of the pocket, jet spray ready. Her heart was beating fast. She knew she mustn't take her eyes off him for a second.

"Good boy, Smiley," she said. Her fingers were slippery with sweat and awkward around the syringe. *I should've practiced this!* she thought. But there'd been no time. She fumbled, then pressed the syringe into a fold of skin behind his ear. "You're the best."

Smiley's yellow eyes glared at her, his tail flicked to and fro like an angry cat's. She took a slow step back, watching him, then another.

"Did you get him?" Ailee whispered.

She turned to face Ailee. "I think so——"

And Smiley sprang.

Nan went down.

Ailee screamed.

Nan wanted to scream too but she couldn't. One large paw was planted on her throat and she could hardly breathe. Time seemed to stop. The sound of the animal's heart was as loud as a drum. His breath was hot and smelled rotten. The long saber teeth were just inches away.

But it was his eyes that had changed most; they glittered strangely. She wouldn't have recognized them.

And she knew he didn't recognize her anymore.

In her mind she heard the training words she'd accidentally teased him with, *"You're the best."* But she had no treats in her pocket this time.

For several seconds nothing moved. It was as if the smilodon were trying to make sense of two competing instincts: affection for his former playmate and the hunting instincts of a wild animal.

Wildness won. The beast opened its enormous jaw.

Nan caught a confused glimpse of huge teeth. Then Will seemed to fall on the smilodon. There was a flash of metal—

The smilodon grunted once and toppled over.

Jerry and DeShawn dragged his heavy body off her. Ailee, tears streaming down her cheeks, helped Nan up.

Will sat on the floor, looking dazed. In his hand he held the long knife he'd carried with him all the way from Drake's galleon.

The blade was red with Smiley's blood.

35

Nan and the team sat silently in the galley the next day. They were all staring at the holographic mountains on the wall, trying not to think about what happened to Smiley. They each had a mug of hot chocolate in their hands, a gift from the kids on Edge Two, who sent it over in a big thermos jug. Arti lay at their feet.

The dead cub and the Edge scientist, Milo Pike, had both been sent to Edge Two with a 'bot escort. DeShawn talked with Doctor Orgel in Kern, who decided Smiley would be t-ported back to Earth, where zoo veterinarians could do an autopsy to see what went wrong.

Nan didn't need an autopsy to know. She felt deeply responsible for Smiley's death. Everybody had warned her he was a wild animal, and she'd treated him as if he were a pet. She should've seen this coming and prevented it.

The only person who seemed to feel worse than she did was Will. His face was full of grief, and he hadn't touched his hot chocolate, something he'd learned to love. She put an arm around his shoulders.

"You saved my life, Will," she whispered. "Keep thinking about that."

"Ailee hath the right of it," Will answered. "I be too bloody-minded."

"I didn't mean it as a criticism, Will," Ailee said. "I think you're very brave. I couldn't have done it."

Jerry said, "I feel as if I should've figured something else out, so we didn't have to use Smiley. But I've run out of ideas."

Maybe Arlo Pike had been right and she didn't belong here, Nan thought. She was a mistake, a nobody, and she'd messed everything up.

DeShawn leaned down to Arti. "Can you read the station monitors from here? I don't feel up to going back into Command just yet."

"Certainly." Arti closed his eyes. "Hmm."

"What is it?" Jerry asked.

"It didn't take the Thogs long to learn nobody was chasing them anymore," Arti said. "A large number of them are gathering openly in the SRL."

"Time to brace ourselves for more power failures," DeShawn advised.

"At present they're just milling around," Arti said. "But I'd estimate there are at least two hundred— Wait. More are coming out of the walls."

Jerry groaned. "Didn't we make *any* kind of dent in those darn Thogs?"

DeShawn stood up. "Might as well go over and take a look. Coming, Jerry? Nan?"

"Sure." Jerry didn't sound too enthusiastic.

Nan said nothing. She didn't care to look at another Thog in her life. They could take over the whole of Oort One for all she cared right now.

"Come on, Nan," Ailee coaxed. "Don't give up now."

"Oh my," Arti said. "I don't think we realized

there were this many Thogs on the station. And they're still coming!''

The boys and Arti left the galley at a fast walk.

"Nan?" Ailee urged. She held out both hands. "Will?"

Will grabbed one hand and let Ailee drag him to his feet. Reluctantly, Nan took the other. They caught up with the guys and the AI in the transfer node between the connector and the SRL.

"I don't think we want to go in there right now," Jerry said quietly, blocking their way into the SRL.

Nan peered around him, and her mouth fell open in shock. The floor of the science module seemed to have been recarpeted. But this carpet, a wall-to-wall thick gray shag, was moving. It made her skin crawl.

"How many do you estimate?" DeShawn asked.

"Several hundred," Arti replied.

"We're in trouble," Jerry said.

Then the gray carpet seemed to ripple; holes appeared through which Nan could see the regular blue-tiled floor of the module.

"What be happening?" Will whispered.

"I think they're forming a giant ball," DeShawn said.

"Now's our last chance, DeShawn!" Jerry said urgently. "Seal off the SRL. Trap them in here, then shut down the life support systems. They need air just as we do. We've got to destroy them once and for all."

"Maybe we could do it." DeShawn sounded doubtful. "There are separate controls for each module in Command. But we've never done such a thing before."

Now the edges of the carpet seemed to be flowing

217

into the middle and a hump was rising. The shape of a ball began to emerge.

"Do it!" Jerry urged.

Nan tuned the boys out and stared at the Thogs. They were still coming, pouring out of the cubicles and the walls, streaming through the transfer node at the team's feet so that she had to pick hers up to avoid brushing against their fur. This many Thogs were surely enough to blow Oort One to pieces. Was that what Milo Pike meant by critical mass?

"That ball is enormous already." Ailee sounded very scared. "DeShawn, I think Jerry's right. We're in real trouble."

And still the Thogs came. How could there possibly have been this many on the station, Nan wondered.

"Hurry!" Jerry yelled.

DeShawn turned back the way they'd come, his shoulders drooping.

"Wait!" Nan said, grabbing hold of DeShawn's arm.

They all stared at her. A lot of things were starting to come together in her mind. She didn't know what they ought to do, but killing off the Thogs before they understood what the aliens were doing didn't seem right—because there was purpose here, she was certain.

"I guess I'm tired of all this killing," she explained. "Okay, so I'm buying into this peace stuff we've been hearing! But hold off for a few more minutes, Jerry. Let's watch."

"Are you crazy?" Jerry asked. "There are enough Thogs to destroy the entire station!"

"And we five with it," Will added.

"No!" Nan yelled. "Wait, I tell you. Wait."

The others seemed so surprised by her outburst that they did as she said and waited.

The Thog ball was a gigantic furry mass in the center of the hall. There must be at least a thousand of the alien creatures in there, she thought. But it had stopped growing; no more Thogs rolled to join it.

"Something's happening," Arti murmured. "But I don't know quite what."

"We're all dead, that's what!" Jerry exclaimed.

"We've got to find out what they're doing," Nan said. "If we don't, this could happen again and doom more people than just us."

"Aye," Will said loyally. "Nan hath the right of it."

The team waited in silence. It was a gamble, and if Nan was wrong, they could lose their lives. Yet something told her to wait and see.

For a long moment after the last Thogs joined the ball, nothing happened. Then Nan noticed that the hair on her arms and the back of her neck was rising, and she saw Will scrubbing at his arms as if he felt it too.

"Arti?" Ailee whispered. "Arti!"

Nan glanced down. The computer dog appeared to have gone into his alien-overload mode. His eyes were glassy and his body so still it was easy to remember he was a machine.

"Not again!" Jerry said.

Arti suddenly shook himself awake. "I'm picking up something extraordinary from the ball."

"What is it? What're you getting?" Nan asked.

"A voice," Arti said. "Quite remarkable."

"One voice?" Ailee asked. "But there're hundreds of them!"

"What does it say?" Nan demanded.

"That doesn't make sense!" Jerry protested. "How could the Thogs speak English?"

"I'm not exactly hearing words," Arti explained. "I'm getting images, concepts. Yet it seems clear enough."

"Is there any way you can let us hear too?" Nan asked.

The computer-dog nodded his head. "Put your hands on me, all of you. I'll try a direct translation relay."

They did as they were told, DeShawn and Ailee looking puzzled, Jerry looking skeptical, and Will looking nervous.

Nan set both hands firmly on the top of Arti's head. When she did so, a tiny voice spoke somewhere deep in her mind.

We are here. We are all here. Where are you?

Jerry's hands flew off Arti and he stared at Nan.

"Be this sorcery?" Will asked. His eyes had gone very big and round.

Nan couldn't explain it to Will because there were no words to tell how she understood, but somehow she knew this was the right thing to be doing.

We need you! the voice said in her mind. *Guide us. We are young. We will help.*

She said out loud, "We'll guide you. But we're young too. How will you help us?"

She tangled her fingers deep in Arti's fur as she spoke. Jerry put his hands back on Arti, and the others did the same.

"Speak to us again!" Nan commanded. "We are the guides! How will you help us?"

We know many things, many, many things, the voice said. *Touch us, you who have bonded. To the bonded we are friends.*

"What're they talking about?" Ailee wondered.

Will shook his head too.

DeShawn looked grim. "There's a threat in that. How do we know who's bonded? And what happens if they decide we're not?"

Jerry asked, "What will you do to those who haven't bonded, as you call it?"

Destroy, the voice said sadly.

The five humans looked at each other again and shook their heads.

"Methinks this be a trap!" Will said.

"No. Wait. I'm beginning to understand," Nan said, remembering what Library told her when Will was sick. "They're parasites and they need to coexist with a host. I think we've found a symbiont."

"But what if we're not the host they've bonded with?" Ailee asked. "They'll destroy us! There are other races in our galaxy. Maybe the Thogs were looking for one of them."

Nan pulled her fingers out of Arti's fur and looked at them. The rash she'd got from touching a Thog was still faintly visible. "Here's the bond," she said.

Jerry took his hands off Arti, and gazed at them too. Then he held them up so Nan could see the little red rash across the inside of his fingers. She nodded and he took hold of one of her hands. Together, they approached the Thog ball.

"Jerry! Nan! Are you certain this is right?" DeShawn asked.

Nan took a deep breath. "I'm certain."

"Yes," Jerry said.

At the same time, they placed their free hands on the ball. It was warm and soft, and a tingle of static electricity flowed up Nan's arm.

Our kind live deep in space, the voice said in Nan's

mind. *We are lonely for those who bond. Guide us and we will help you.*

Nan said, "If you can hear me, wait. We'll get help from the elders of our kind. They'll know how to go on from here."

The voices were silent after that. Gradually the ball of Thogs broke down as Thogs left the heap. There was a new orderliness in their movement, and none of them fled away from the humans. Nan, Jerry, Will, Ailee, and DeShawn stood with their arms around each other, watching.

Nan knew the Thogs would come back when humans called. The two races had bonded, and both would benefit.

36

"**I** feel bad about the Thogs we killed before we understood," DeShawn said to Jerry.

They were standing by Airlock A, just before the team left Oort One. Jerry glanced down at his hands. The rash was fading already.

DeShawn added, "I'll never forget you or what you did for us, Jerry."

Jerry shook DeShawn's hand. This guy from the future had proved he had grit. He was going to miss DeShawn. He was about to say, *And I'll never forget you either.* But then he remembered what they'd been told at the start: They wouldn't be allowed to take their memories back with them.

Instead, he said, "De nada, friend."

Jerry, Ailee, Nan, and Will went into the shuttle. Ailee had a large carrier with the remaining cats in it. DeShawn and Arti stayed on Oort One to monitor comets and aliens until the scientists back in Kern decided what to do.

From Edge Two, the little group made the jumps back from t-port to t-port, finally emerging into brilliant sunshine on the lawn of the operations center in Kern. Jerry blinked and saw Doctor Cee, Doctor Orgel, and Master Lobo waiting for them. The operation's experts had their arms full of pink and purple flower chains which they draped around the team's necks like the leis visitors are given in Hawaii.

"What a priceless gift you've given humankind!" Doctor Orgel said, shaking Nan's hand. "Who knows what advances we'll make now in cooperation with the Thogemags, thanks to you, Nan."

Doctor Cee gave Jerry a hug. "You were truly magnificent!"

"I'm proud of you. You were all tigers!" Master Lobo said, patting Will on the shoulder.

A woman and a younger girl came running up to Ailee and hugged her. For a few minutes, everybody stood around, talking on the lawn.

"I'm going to be leaving Kern with my family immediately after the banquet," Ailee said, turning to Jerry.

It was even harder to know what to say to Ailee than it had been to DeShawn. Once or twice while they were on Oort One, Jerry had thought of saying something about how much he liked her. Now he was kind of glad he hadn't. He wanted to thank her for her help, tell her how much he valued her friendship, and—what? Hope he met her again? Because that was the problem. What could he say to someone he not only was never going to see again, but who wasn't even born when he was alive?

Instead he said, "Goodbye. I'll miss you."

"Goodbye, Jerry. I'll miss you too." She leaned over and kissed him on the cheek.

He blushed and turned away.

Master Lobo put his arms around Nan's and Will's shoulders, and steered them inside the building.

Serena Cee turned to Jerry. "There's always a let-down feeling at the end of an adventure, Jerry. That's quite natural.''

''It was great to be in charge, nobody telling me it was too risky for my health,'' Jerry said. ''I feel good about what we did, but I also feel sad.''

''Yes,'' she said. ''That's why we want you all to talk about the mission tonight at the banquet. Experiences like these need to be discussed together, the good parts and the bad.''

''What's the point?'' Jerry said. ''You told us we'd forget about everything when we go home.''

''It's even more important that you talk it out before you forget,'' Doctor Cee said.

''And it's better for all of us that we don't know our futures,'' Doctor Orgel added.

The morning after the feast, Jerry, Nan, and Will stood in the room with the white carpet where they'd first arrived. Doctor Cee, Doctor Orgel, and Master Lobo were with them.

Will was going to make the return trip through the time tunnel first. This morning he wore tights, a quilted doublet that looked old and battered, and a faded black velvet hat crammed down over his ears; these were the clothes he'd been wearing when they yanked him. His knife was again tucked into his leather belt. A 'bot would go with him as far as the moment when he stepped out onto the deck of the *Golden Hind* in 1579.

Nan hugged Will to her and for a moment neither of them spoke.

''Enjoy the rest of Drake's round-the-world voyage, Will,'' Nan said. Then she turned and went quickly out of the room.

Jerry knew she was afraid of crying in front of them

and looking like a baby. The truth was, he felt like crying too, but guys didn't break down like that. At least, not in public. He was going to miss Will's friendly grin and his eager appetite for adventure.

"This be a beauteous world," Will said. "I shall greatly miss it."

"We'll miss you too, Will," Doctor Cee said gently.

Master Lobo said, "Your mind may forget what you learned here, but I think your muscles will remember how to deal with bullies." He mimed a karate kick.

"And in your heart you'll know you helped our world," Doctor Cee added. "You are one of our heroes."

Jerry and Will shook hands.

"Enjoy the rest of your life, Will," Jerry said. "Go up to London and see the Queen. Catch a couple of plays. Some of the new playwrights are pretty awesome."

"Yet one comfort there be in this sad parting," Will said, flashing his mischievous grin. "Upon my return, I shall eat red meat every day!"

Jerry laughed and gave Will the thumbs up sign. "No more green things, Will!"

Serena Cee touched the wall panel and an electric blue light began to spin its way up in front of them. The humming sound Jerry remembered started.

Waving, Will stepped jauntily into the tunnel.

And then he was gone. The blue light vanished.

"Nice kid," Jerry said. "He deserves a long and happy life."

The project scientists said nothing.

"By the way," he said. "How did he show the grit that made you pick him?"

"He's going to save Drake's life when a native in Mindanao tries to stab him," Doctor Orgel said.

"Cool. And will Drake make him his page, like Will wants?" Jerry realized suddenly that the scientists looked uncomfortable with his questions. "What's wrong?"

"I'm afraid Will isn't going to live long after he saves his captain," Master Lobo explained. "He'll be knocked overboard when the *Golden Hind* strikes a reef. He's going to drown."

"But that's unfair!" Jerry protested. "Will deserves much better than that!"

"We understand he was your friend," Doctor Cee said. "We all liked Will too."

"It was hard not to," Master Lobo said. "Such a merry boy."

Jerry thought about Will's future. Sure, in real life rotten things happened to nice kids. Everybody knew that. But it just seemed so unfair that Will could come safely through everything that had happened on Oort One and then drown. It clouded everything for Jerry.

"Cheer up, Jerry," Doctor Cee said. "Don't take it so hard. I can tell you this. It'll happen very quickly and Will won't suffer."

"Not good enough," he said. "I feel now as if there's nothing worth doing any more. A stupid accident can wipe everything out."

Doctor Orgel smiled. "You yourself have a long and splendid career ahead of you, Gerald Vanderburg."

As if I care right now, he thought bitterly.

"Don't you want to know?" Doctor Cee asked, green eyes sparkling, when he didn't say anything.

"So tell me. You won't let me remember it when

I go back, anyway,'' Jerry said. Maybe it would take his mind off Will.

"You're going to make a very important break-through in artificial intelligence,'' Doctor Orgel said. "Without your pioneering work, we wouldn't have had CenCom or an Arti to send up with you.''

"Work that you did—I mean, are going to do!—under very difficult circumstances,'' Master Lobo added.

"I'm responsible for there being such a thing as a computer-dog some day?'' Jerry asked. Then he laughed. "That's weird. I think I might just manage to remember the dog!''

"There are some hard times coming in your future,'' Doctor Cee said seriously. "Today we know it as the Time of Troubles. But wonderful people from all walks of life will perform great heroic service to pull the world through. You're going to be one of them.''

She wasn't joking, Jerry saw.

"Thanks for telling me that,'' he said. But even knowing he was going to be a hero didn't help him get over the sadness of Will's bad fortune.

"Time to prepare for your own return, Jerry,'' Master Lobo said. "I'll go find Nan.'' He went out of the room.

"You still look sad,'' Doctor Cee commented.

"Why didn't you keep Will here?'' Jerry challenged. He was starting to feel angry again. "Why did you send him back knowing what'll happen to him?''

Doctor Cee gazed at him. "We can't interfere with history, Jerry.''

"It would create a time paradox,'' Doctor Orgel

228

said. "And you understand what a mess that would make."

It was a horrible fate for poor Will. And these future scientists, with all their knowledge and technology, were going to stand by and let it happen because of a stupid time paradox. Jerry understood the idea: If you went back in history and killed your grandfather, then your father wouldn't get born and there wouldn't be a you to go back and kill your grandfather in the first place. It meant you couldn't mess with what was supposed to happen. But it was grossly unfair.

Then he had an idea.

"What if you yanked him again," he said. "Just at the moment that he goes under the waves? It wouldn't disturb the time line if he were already supposed to be dead, would it? You could bring him back here with no paradox at all."

Doctor Cee and Doctor Orgel looked at each other for a moment, thinking over Jerry's idea.

"We'd have to be careful. Wait till the very last second," Orgel said. "And we'd need to have a medibot in the tunnel to revive him from drowning. But perhaps it wouldn't cause a very big paradox. A few fish might go hungry, a few birds that would've eaten the fish." Orgel paused as if he were thinking about it, then went on. "And then there's the problem of restoring his memory after we yank him back here—"

"You given us a wonderful idea, Jerry," Doctor Cee said. "We'd love to have Will back here with us. We'll do our very best, but I can't guarantee anything."

"Great! Thanks!" Jerry was elated. "I'm sure you can do it!" Then he thought of something else and had to laugh. "But now poor Will's going to face a lifetime of eating green things!"

37

Nan walked out into the garden. She couldn't stay in the room to watch Will leave because she was afraid she'd cry. Grampa Hong's *I Ching* predictions had been right; it had all turned out okay in the end. But she couldn't help feeling sad at leaving, saying goodbye to friends, not knowing what was going to happen about the brand new symbiont she'd discovered, losing Smiley.

It was good they'd had a chance to talk it out at the banquet. She'd known from the start they were dealing with a dangerous animal in the smilodon, and nobody could've predicted how long they could work with him. All the project scientists yesterday had told her how proud they were of what she'd done, and that was great to hear, but none of it made up for the death of Smiley.

Somewhere a 'bot was mowing the grass and she could smell the fresh scent. It had been a grand adventure, but now she must go back to Oak House. Or worse, juvenile hall. Whatever Will and Jerry went back to, they knew they'd been picked because they would be important some day. They were going to do great things. But she was just Nan the Nobody, here by mistake.

"You seem sad."

She glanced round to see Doctor Arlo Pike. The thin scientist always looked serious, but today he didn't seem quite as angry at her as usual. Maybe the news about his brother had made him think twice.

Nan shrugged. "I'm not looking forward to going home."

He nodded as if he understood. Then he said, "I owe you and all the team my personal thanks. You saved my brother's life. Milo's hasty, quick-tempered, a lot like me."

To her amazement, Pike actually smiled.

Then he turned serious again. "We were very close as boys, and we both devoted our lives to science. But Milo's work took him to Edge Two as a teen, and he never returned while it was still possible for him to t-port. I haven't seen him for a very long time, and probably will never see him in person again. Maybe you can understand how that made me jealous of kids who can t-port with ease?"

"Yeah, I guess I can understand," Nan said.

"I owe you an apology too," he said.

This unusual niceness was making her uncomfortable. He really was a bore when he was trying to be nice. She was beginning to think she preferred the grumpy version of Doctor Arlo Pike. At least she knew how to deal with him.

"Come with me, please," Pike said.

He headed across the lawn to the t-port booth. Nan followed him. When he opened the door and stepped inside, then held the door for her, she was astonished.

"Are you sure?" she asked. "Won't you get a headache?"

"This is something I must do," he said.

Pike entered a code into the pad, the back wall

turned misty and they stepped through together. They came out of the booth in front of the archway to the zoo where she'd first seen the adult female smilodon.

"I want to show you something," Pike said, leading the way down the path through the humid tropical forest.

Dodo birds peered shyly at them under the trees, and a dire wolf slunk away into the ferns as they passed. A woolly mammoth trumpeted from a green pool.

"Where are we going?" Nan asked.

The tall scientist shook his head, then he seemed to regret it. He held his head between his hands for a moment and closed his eyes. That must be some huge headache from t-porting, she thought. Why had he risked it?

A moment later, he stopped by the sign where Nan had first read the information about *Smilodon Californicus*.

"What—" she began.

"Wait," he said, holding up his hand.

They waited. After a while, the fronds of a huge green tree fern rustled and the female smilodon emerged and bent her neck to drink at a pool. The female looked so like Smiley that it brought a flood of memories. To Nan's mind, the saber-toothed tiger was the most magnificent animal that had ever existed.

"She's expecting another cub," Doctor Pike said. "I thought it might help you to know."

There was a dry lump in Nan's throat. "It does."

"This one will be a female," he added. "Maybe we'll name her 'Nan.' "

She smiled, a bit shakily. "I'd be honored."

Pike took her arm and led her to a bench where

they could sit and watch the smilodon. She glanced at him and saw his face was pale. When he thought she wasn't watching, he pressed his hands to his temples again. After a while, the larger male smilodon came out of the trees to join his mate and stood yawning, exposing the enormous dagger teeth. They were a glorious pair.

"And I also owe you an explanation," Pike said. "Nan Smith, tell me what your full name is."

Surprised, Nan forgot the smilodons to stare at him. "Why?"

"Please. It's important."

"Well, Smith was my stepfather's name," she began slowly. "But my real name is Shenandoah Whitecrow."

Pike sighed and closed his eyes for a second. "I should've listened to Serena from the first," he said. "She told me, the AIs don't make mistakes."

"You mean, I'm not here by mistake? Arti *meant* to snatch me?" Nan asked.

"Yes," he said.

"But I'm a nobody. You told me that!"

"I was wrong," Pike replied. He stood up again. "There's something else I want you to see."

This time he took her down a path they hadn't taken on the other visit. It opened out on a little hill overlooking a peaceful lake; a herd of deer and their fawns grazed on the hill, and bright birds flashed over the water.

"Look," he said, pointing.

Nan saw a small white-painted gazebo where visitors could rest and enjoy the view. There was a bronze statue in front of the gazebo. She went over and studied it. An old woman with long braided hair and a kind face shielded her eyes with one hand as she seemed to look out over the water; in one arm she cradled a tiny wolf cub. The mother wolf leaned against her skirts, gazing up at her, and two rabbits and a fox snuggled on her other side. The animals looked almost real; only the glint of sunlight on the dark metal told her they weren't. On the statue's shoulders were two birds, one a crow made of bronze, the other a dove, alive and preening its feathers in the sunshine.

"Read the sign," Pike said.

Nan did as she was told. *"Shenandoah White-crow,"* she read, and stopped. "What?"

"Keep reading," Pike said.

"She loved and saved so many animals," Nan finished. The last words were hard to see because there were suddenly tears getting in the way.

"Is that really me?" she asked, finally.

Pike nodded. "When I realized how important you were to the team," he said softly, "I made a thorough search of the historical records of the twenty-first century, as I should've done right from the start. The name 'Nan Smith' didn't appear anywhere. But Shenandoah Whitecrow is famous, as you can see."

Nan stared at him, biting her lip to stop it from trembling.

"You're going to become one of the Ten Thousand Heroes that we talked about at the banquet," he added. "You're responsible for saving hundreds of species of animals from extinction."

She couldn't think of a thing to say.

"Miss Whitecrow," Doctor Pike said at last, "I'm honored to meet you."

He held out his hand to her and she took it. Pike gazed at her for a moment as if he were memorizing her face, then he let her hand go.

They walked back to the zoo's entrance in silence. The sun was low in the sky now. As the light faded, one of the comets streaming toward Earth from the Oort Cloud became visible, a gaudy firework with a long, luminous tail. It was comforting to know De-Shawn had probably monitored that one and decided it was going to miss.

"It's getting late," Pike said. "And you have to get back. I won't t-port with you. I'll take the slower way."

She glanced at him and saw sweat beading on his forehead. His mouth was tight with the fierce headache she knew he must have, but all the anger and irritation that she usually read in his face had drained away.

"Thanks for telling me that, Doctor Pike," she said. "I'm ready to go back to my own time now."

"You understand," he said gently, "we can't allow you to remember a word of what I've just said."

38

Nan and Jerry waved good-bye to the scientists in the room with the white carpet. Holding each other's hand, they stepped into the spinning blue light.

The familiar motion sickness caught her almost immediately, but she remembered this time to keep walking, pulling Jerry along through the misty tunnel. Walking helped, as Arti had told them the first time. It felt odd to be wearing her own clothes again, faded jeans and red sweater, not the sky blue jumpsuit with the Operation Hourglass logo on it.

"I'm not going to forget any of this adventure," Jerry said. "Are you?"

" 'Course not," she said.

The last thing Doctor Cee had done was give them each an amnesiac, to make them forget their adventures in 2345. It didn't seem to be working yet. Nan agreed with Jerry; it would be a shame to forget the things they'd done, the great times they'd had. They both understood Doctor Cee's reasons, but Nan figured they could keep a secret. They wouldn't tell anybody at all that they'd been to the future. Who'd believe them anyway?

"Remember the Thogs," Jerry said, slowing down. "Remember the Thogs. Remember the Thogs."

"What're you doing?" she asked. The hot, metallic smell in the tunnel made her stomach feel queasy. "Keep walking, Jerry!"

"It's a mantra against forgetting," he said. "Remember the Thogs. Remember the Thogs."

"I'd rather remember Smiley!" she grumbled.

The tunnel glowed red behind them and blue ahead. This time, the air was filled with eerie noises, howls, shrieks, like a soundtrack played backwards. She shivered and tugged Jerry's arm to get him to walk faster.

"Remember the Thogs," Jerry muttered. "We can do it, Nan. Remember the Thogs. Remember the—"

Suddenly, Nan felt a push, as if she'd been shoved off a moving train.

"—dog," Jerry was saying.

"What?" Nan stared round at the deserted street. For a moment she'd forgotten where she was. She must've been daydreaming.

"Remember my dog!" Jerry said.

It was getting late; the street lamps—the ones nobody had wrecked yet anyway—were coming on. She didn't want to be here when it got totally dark. At night, this part of Santa Marta belonged completely to the gangs.

"Huh?" Jerry said. He was rubbing his head as if he had a headache. "Oh. Yes. I can't go without my dog."

Behind them, she heard a bark, and Jerry's big red setter raced up, almost knocking Jerry down in its eagerness.

"Rufus, you old dingbat!" Jerry said. "I was worried about you. Don't ever run away again."

The dog licked Jerry's face.

Something fluttered in Nan's mind as she watched,

something she thought she ought to remember. She waited a second. Nothing came back.

"What time is it?" Jerry asked.

She lifted her arm before she remembered she wasn't wearing a watch. The flashlight in her pocket bumped against her hip. "I dunno. Late."

There was a long pale scar on the inside of her arm. She pushed her sleeve up and stared at it. Cat scratch, she thought. Then she frowned. When had Tiger done that? She'd have noticed if the Oak House cat had given her a scratch as big as that. How could she have got such a scar?

"This is a wonderful old part of town, isn't it?" Jerry said suddenly.

Nan glanced at him, expecting to see him wink or something. But she realized he wasn't making a joke; he meant what he said.

"I mean, look at the old houses. They must be at least a hundred years old," he said. "And the interesting shape of the street lamps. Look at that one!"

The bump on his head must've done more damage than she'd realized. Nan glanced over to where he was pointing. She'd never paid attention to the shape of the street lamps before; now she saw that the bulbs on top were shaped like flames, and their light was a warm amber. The light poles were made of cast iron, ribbed and decorated with ivy vines curled around them. The funny thing was, Jerry was right. They were wonderful.

She looked up. The sky was a deep, violet blue, with just a touch of pink still in the west where the sun had set. Stars were starting to show; she could see Venus already, the evening star, and a pale sliver of new moon was just rising over the rooftops. *And somewhere out there is the Oort Cloud. . . .*

Where did that thought come from? Even more surprising, she found she knew what the Oort Cloud was, and where. Maybe it was something she'd seen in a *Star Trek* episode. Wherever the idea came from, it made her feel happy.

She flung her arms out wide.

"Hello world!" she yelled. "This is Shenandoah Whitecrow ready to take on anything you can send!"

Now it was Jerry's turn to stare at her as if she'd gone crazy. She didn't care. But it startled her a bit that she'd used her full name. Well, why not? Hadn't her roomie told her it was nice? Maybe she should start being proud of it.

"I have to be getting home," Jerry said. "My mom'll be worried. She fusses over me too much. I'm going to have to do something about that soon. I'll be going away to university and I can look out for myself. But those guys stole my new racing bike, so I guess I'll need to take a bus. Do you think they'll let me take my dog on a bus?"

"I doubt it," she said. "We could call a taxi for you, if you have any money."

He groaned. "I don't. But my dad will pay if a taxi brings me home."

"Cool," she said. "Look. There's a phone over there. I have a quarter in my pocket. If the phone's working, I'll call a cab for you."

It was, and she did. While they waited for the cab to come, Nan found herself humming, something she almost never did. What's wrong with me tonight? she wondered. But it wasn't wrong; it felt absolutely right.

The headlights of the cab turned the corner onto the street where they stood.

"Can I give you a lift home, Nan?" Jerry asked.

"Nah," she said. "I'll take the bus."

The cab pulled up at the curb and Jerry and Rufus scrambled inside. Jerry gave the driver an address that Nan recognized as being on the fancy side of Santa Marta. Then he pulled a small pad and a stub of pencil from a pocket and scribbled something down. As the driver started the cab again, Jerry held a scrap of paper out the window.

"Give me a call sometime, Nan," he said. "I'm grateful to you for helping me. I'd like to stay in touch."

"Sure." She took the paper, wondering what they would have in common to talk about, a rich kid and a runaway. Yet somehow she had a feeling they might manage to find something. She waved until the cab turned the corner out of sight.

There was one more quarter in her pocket. She walked back to the phone booth and entered a number. She had to speak to the woman at the desk, who had to call her supervisor, and it took a while before they carried the phone down to his room. The sky was completely dark by the time he answered.

"Grampa?" she said. "This is Shenandoah. I know it's late. I just had to tell you. I'm going back to Oak House. Running away won't help. And I'm going to work harder in school. I'll try to make something of my life. What happened to me? I don't know, Grampa. I just realized I wanted to do it, I guess."

She gazed up at the sky like black velvet with a sprinkling of diamonds. The Big Dipper was directly overhead.

"I love you, Grampa," she said, putting the phone down.

Tonight she thought the constellation looked more like an animal than a dipper. A bear, maybe. Or a tiger made of light. A tiger in the sky. Something about that idea made her want to laugh and cry at the same time.

Walking toward the bus stop, she realized she'd never felt so full of joy in her life.

New York Times bestselling author

DAVID BRIN'S
OUT OF TIME

continues in August 1999 with

ᵀᴴᴱ GAME ᴼᶠ WORLDS

BY ROGER MACBRIDE ALLEN

It's the year 2345...Young heroes yanked from the twentieth century and beyond must fight an enemy more skilled, cunning, and dangerous than they ever imagined. But these young heroes are the world's only hope...

Adam O'Conner is no stranger to trouble. His most recent stunt—setting off firecrackers in a teacher's car—has landed him a school suspension, 1990s style. But even Adam can't have predicted the brand of trouble that awaits him far in the future, when he's yanked out of time to lead a historic meeting between humans and the alien K'lugu and Devlins. Adam is about to encounter trouble on a grand scale. Or will he display the "grit" that only a select few in his generation possess? Will he become the hero that he is destined to be?

DBG 0399

FREE! FREE! FREE!
DAVID BRIN'S
OUT OF TIME
P O S T E R   O F F E R

Avon Books is pleased you've chosen the exciting new **OUT OF TIME** series by *New York Times* bestselling author DAVID BRIN and a team of highly acclaimed science fiction writers. As our welcome gift to you, we'd like to send you a dynamic full color poster illustrating this original science fiction adventure series—absolutely FREE! Just fill out the coupon below, and send it to us with proof of purchase (sales receipts) of: *Yanked* (on sale in June 1999), *Tiger in the Sky* (on sale in July 1999), and *The Game of Worlds* (on sale in August 1999) and we'll rush a poster your way.

Void where prohibited by law.

- -

Mail to:
Avon Books, Dept. BP, P.O. Box 767, Dresden, TN 38225

Name_____

Address_____

City_____

State/Zip_____

DBP 0399